Author's Note

Mishbil's fictional difficulties have an exact counterpart on our globe. The pre-Hispanic Chimu Indians of northwest Peru excavated a complex canal system about 700 years ago that extended 50 miles to link two separate drainage basins. Movements of the earth's crust gradually thwarted their astonishing hydraulic engineering and, after years of painful redigging, the system's deathblow was finally delivered by torrential rains around 1300 A.D.

That phenomenon is known nowadays as El Niño. Tornados in California, brush fires in Australia, drought in Indonesia, devastating downpours in Ecuador and coastal Peru—all can be credited to a rare warming of surface waters in the eastern equatorial Pacific.

This book was written in a particularly bad El Niño year. As much as 300 percent more rainfall devastated some countries; a headline in the *Washington Post* reads, "Five Months of Torrents Swamp Peruvian Desert." The author is certain this timing is a coincidence.

—B.W.C.

THE
DRAGON
OF
MISHBIL

B.W. CLOUGH

DAW BOOKS, INC.
DONALD A. WOLLHEIM, PUBLISHER

1633 Broadway, New York, NY 10019

DAW Collectors' Book No. 645

DEDICATION

To Larry, my most fervent fan.

First Printing, September 1985

1 2 3 4 5 6 7 8 9

Printed in U.S.A.

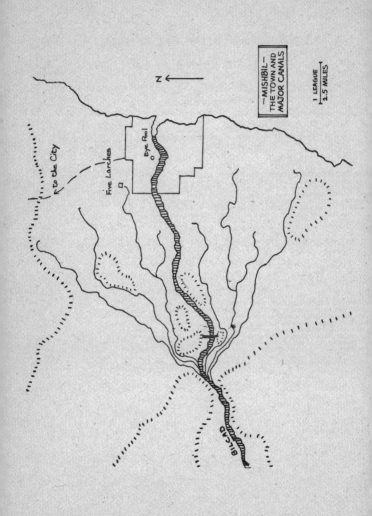

No man, I suppose, is tempted to every sin. It so happens that the impulse which makes men gamble has been left out of my make-up; and, no doubt, I pay for this by lacking some good impulse of which it is the excess or perversion.

C.S. Lewis

Chapter 1: Mid Summer Day

The rule for wishes at the Temple of the Sun is that the petition must be made by the concerned party only. Farmers approach the deity one by one to wish for good harvesting weather, though the warmth that ripens the grain would shine equally on all. And though a pregnant woman may thank the goddess Ennelith for her fertility, if she wishes a babe of one sex or the other she must carefully climb the winding road—it is steep, up the scarp to the Upper City—to make the wish, and neither husband nor parent may make the request in her place.

Therefore, when Zaryas-yu Borletsikan, ruling princess of Mishbil, presented her offering and wish Mid Summer Day she knew the voyage north might well be in vain. "Yet what could I have done?" she demanded of the priestess. "Brought the entire population of my city along to wish?"

"You are their mediator before the god," the holy woman replied. "And it is a very propitious day. Let us make the offering and see."

No blood may be shed at the altar of the Lord of Life, so Zaryas had brought eight red porcelain jars of aromatic gums and spices. Her retinue waited behind while she and the priestess approached the central altar. Only Zaryas' firm booted step echoed back from the towering golden dome above the circular sanctuary, for the priestess wore soft leather slippers. As they came near, the presence of the deity seemed to press on her soul silent and heavy and full of light, like massive gold. She tried to tread more quietly, with partial success.

In awed silence she watched the perfumes, worth far more than silver, poured out onto the altar. Sweet blue smoke billowed up in heady clouds, making her sneeze, but the priestess' steady gaze did not waver from the flames. Fueled by the oily essences the fire leaped, roaring high above their heads, shooting out a fountain of gold sparks and illuminating the great sanctuary like a lightning bolt. Zaryas retreated a pace or two and wiped her streaming eyes with a silk handkerchief.

Without turning her head the priestess said, "Repeat your wish, please."

"That the canals of Mishbil conduct water again," Zaryas said in a thick voice.

For a long moment the crackle of flame was the only reply. Then the priestess turned away and Zaryas saw the doubt in her face. "The omens are clouded, princess," she told Zaryas. "Your wish shall be granted, but not as you expect."

"That, alas, will not do." Zaryas coughed and

rubbed her burning eyes with thumb and fore-finger. "Should I have wished simply for the canals and river to flow as they used to?"

"To answer that I need not consult the Sun," the priestess said. "Times, like rivers, never turn back. You and your city must go forward."

"When the wind fails, unship your oars," Zaryas quoted the proverb to her aides. So her next call was at the Palace of the Shan King. In contrast to the archaic severity of the Temple beside it, the Palace was a rambling complex of interconnected halls and chambers. Every possible style of building was manifested in exuberant glory, unified only by the purity of polished white marble and the favorite triple-arched windows. Every year at winter solstice Zaryas journeyed here to present her King with an account of the year's doings. But she had never deigned to master the intricacies of the Palace maze. "Your own fault," she often told King Varim. "Appointing an absent-minded little snip to run Mishbil for you!" The incongruity of this always made the King laugh, for both knew Zaryas never forgot or forgave anything.

The Shan King's schedule that day was full. In an excess of nepotism a minister had staffed his department entirely with relatives, and the King had to decide how many of them to execute. But by pleading emergency Zaryas was allotted a few moments between appointments. The monarch heard his viceroy's tale with interest. The Crystal Crown gleamed so white and luminous on his brow that all the life in the pale old face seemed to be draining upward. Varim looked far more worn than he had six short months ago. But, mindful of time constraints, Zaryas kept to her story.

"I personally cannot help you," the King told her when she had done. "My feeble powers are only over man."

"Then give me magi, Your Majesty," Zaryas said. "Strong hydromants to command the waters to flow rightly, or pirolurges to scorch the channels open again. My own water-wizards have thrown up their hands in despair!"

"Truly? Then you must be desperate indeed," the Shan King sighed. For Mishbil is noted for its hydromants. "The Chamberlain will conduct you to the Master Magus right away. Zarlim has promoted some notable magi recently out of the apprentice ranks. Have him invite you to dine. The magi's cook makes up in succulence what their table lacks in substance."

The shift to homelier topics allowed Zaryas to demand, "And what of you, Varim, have you been eating properly?"

The old King sighed again. "Kings are not long-lived in Averidan," he said.

"Nonsense!" Zaryas said robustly. "You've long, lecherous years in you yet. Why, if it weren't for your wife I'd take you on myself."

Once, Varim would have laughed aloud at that. Now he chuckled. "Executing people tires me, that's all," he declared. "You mustn't tempt an absolute despot, dear Zaryas. I might give way and include the Lady in this latest batch of lapidations. Now run along with you, I have more unpleasant business."

The most high-ranking Chamberlain conducted Zaryas and her party to the magi. Down dozens of wide solemn corridors they went, twisting and turning, up stairs and down, until they lost their bearings entirely. Zaryas, an inveterate gambler herself, grumbled that they were being led by circuitous routes on a wager. But at last they were shown into an open courtyard enclosed by colonnades of gray marble. On benches set near the circular scrying pool sat several men in long robes of dark red linen, with matching peaked and lappetted caps on their heads. They rose to greet Zaryas, laying aside their writing tablets.

"Zarlim, Master Magus," she greeted the eldest, remembering him from other occasions.

"Zaryas-yu, princess of Mishbil," the stout old magus returned. "These are my assistants, Xerlanthor and Xantallon." To either side the younger magi bowed to her. "Sit, and tell us your business."

Zaryas came forward to take the offered bench, and gasped in horror. Level with the pavement, lined with pure black marble, and brimful with limpid water, the pool seemed to be an endless shaft, piercing the uttermost depths of the earth. The sudden vertigo was so terrible she felt her head spin. But seeing her distress the Magus thrust the handle of his wide fan into the water, and the concentric ripples revealed the pool was only ankle-deep.

Furious at this demonstration of weakness Zaryas demanded, "Is it enchanted?"

"Not at all," the Magus said. "The days when such pools were used for scrying are past."

"Mirrors are easier to carry around," Xantallon explained kindly. He was a prodigiously tall and lean young man whom Zaryas had not met before, though from his narrow hawk-face she judged he was a native of Mishbil. He affected a limp black mustache which veiled his mouth, not being long enough to sweep to either side yet. Zaryas did not want anyone's sympathy, and inwardly seething sat down on the offered seat to begin her tale for the second time that day:

"You know, of course, of the difficulties we've been having with the Bilcad River. Our sorrow, the Dragon of Mishbil—but our only source of water in the desert south. Thousands of canals conduct the river water to the fields, and so we live."

"Generations of magi helped plan and dig those canals," the Magus reminded her.

Taking the hint Zaryas hastened to her point. "For decades there has been less and less water in the river," she continued. "We've dug and redug the canals year by year. This spring the ultimate disaster befell us. The Bilcad's waters no longer reach the canal mouths. Our canals are dry, our fields dust, our crops sere."

Xantallon rubbed long dry hands together. "I'd wager my staff," he said, "that it's not less water, but a deeper channel the river has cut for itself. Do you realize what that might prove?"

"You mean the theory that the entire seacoast of Averidan is rising?" Xerlanthor asked. "It's still nothing but speculation, riddled with inconsistencies. For example, why doesn't our shoreline here to the north rise also?"

"Several factors could account for that," Xantallon argued. "What if sand is lighter than earth? What if earth currents behave as ocean currents do, swerving in toward the shoreline at one point only? Like this—" Taking the waxen tablet up he began to sketch, his mustache quivering with scholarly excitement, while Xerlanthor watched over his shoulder.

Snatching at her scattered wits Zaryas brought her hand down in a resounding blow on the bench beside her. "Do you mean to say you magi knew this would happen?" she demanded. "Why did no one inform me? Mishbil may starve next winter!"

The younger magi started, but their Master blinked at Zaryas with mild eyes. "This theory has been current in magian circles for twelve hundred years," he said. "It was propounded by geomants to account for certain curious fluxes in the earth currents. Even if it's correct the land rises very slowly—at most, a handspan every generation or so. The dangers are cumulative, of course, but it was hardly an urgent peril."

"I suppose not," Zaryas conceded. She frowned at the smiling pool of water before her. "The unfairness of it," she sighed. "A trouble so many eons in the brewing, descending in my time."

Xerlanthor glanced up and smiled at her, a

charming smile that warmed and heartened like a sip of plum brandy. "Are you less able to deal with it than your predecessors?" he asked.

"Of course not!" She looked more closely at him. This young magus was of a different breed entirely than his fellows, solid, rosy, and ever so slightly plump, like a ripening plum. Under the red cap a round, merry face smiled, the countenance of one who has always had fortune's favor. She judged he was just past thirty—the age the demigod Shan Vir-yan had been when he founded Averidan. Magi are dreamers, but Xerlanthor's intelligent dark eyes saw practicality, noted everything about her from the braided black hair flecked prematurely with gray to her plain yet vivid countenance, right down to her sensible red hobnailed traveling boots. Here, it seemed, was a courage and will that matched her own. "I like your spirit," she declared. "A few more like you and we'll deal with it indeed."

Chapter 2: 2 Arbas

By tradition all viceroys in Averidan are appointed by the Shan King, who is ineluctably bound to choose the wise and competent. Varim had selected Zaryas four years ago. "No one at twenty-five years of age has any wisdom," she had pointed out. "Why choose me?"

He had stared into her eyes so piercingly she was reminded of the uncomfortable proverb, that the Shan King reads hearts. "My dear princess," he chuckled. "No one is ever told why they are chosen. You will be an entirely satisfactory ruler of Mishbil—I *know*." And since that was the first time anyone had given her the honorific "princess" she had, flustered, acquiesced.

And the King had been right. With the terrifying efficiency she had once devoted to the family silk-dye business she ran Mishbil, cosseting and chastising, nourishing and directing, so that the insalubrious desert city was the envy of Averidan. To be balked now by an uncooperative river was not only intolerable, but a challenge, a wager

thrown down by hostile nature. Zaryas intended
to win.

The next morning she set out well-satisfied
with the beginning she had made. With her city
and all its people at stake Zaryas had half-
persuaded, half-bullied the Master Magus to give
the crisis his personal attention. With him would
come ten other magi, specialists in the earth and
air and water that lay at the heart of the trouble.
Even a restless night of magian hospitality—for
magi hold ideas, particularly magic ideas, in higher
regard than practical matters like the softness of
mattresses or the warmth of bath water—did not
dampen her spirit.

They rose in the milky gray coolness of dawn.
Pearl-colored mist veiled the harbor as they
walked down the main road to the Lower City.
In flat Mishbil the occasional fog spreads out
even and woolly, like a quilt. But here the morning vapors flowed down to collect in the valleys,
looking to Zaryas like fish-sauce poured over porridge. Her ship, the *Silver Gull,* would sail on
the early tide.

The great bronze gate to the Lower City was
just being unbarred for the day. The gate war-
dens groaned and strained at the wheels that
loosened the upper and lower bolts. A chattering
bright-clad crowd surged impatiently out the moment the gate was opened, only to meet an iden-
tically noisy and vivid crowd outside waiting to
get in. The resulting conflict resembled a battle
of demented parrots. Zaryas and the magi held
aloof until the shoving arguments and curses about

trodden toes or upset pots had subsided. Then with dignity intact they passed through.

The Shan King had rightly warned her of scanty magi meals, and now Zaryas sent her maid to buy a sackful of oranges from a street-vendor. When she offered fruit to her companions most of the magi politely declined. But Xerlanthor took one, and by threatening to throw peels and pips induced his friend Xantallon to accept one too. "Though food is simply fuel," Xantallon grumbled, "we Shan think entirely too much about eating."

"So long as we must stoke our fires, why not do so pleasantly?" Xerlanthor demanded. "Besides, it's impolite to turn down a present."

"If you don't care for oranges," Zaryas laughed, "give it back again to your friend." She turned from Xantallon to Xerlanthor and added, "That is if *you* wish it."

Xerlanthor sighed, taking the rejected fruit from his friend and peeling it with deft fingers. "What I wish for I always get," he remarked. He shot a rougish dark glance at her, as if to say he knew his own wishes perfectly well. Since magi profess moderation in worldly pursuits Zaryas should have been startled, but with a tingle of pleasant warmth found she was not.

All the City's ancient streets wound eventually downhill to the harbor. The stone quays and piers had been extended and rebuilt so many times over the centuries that the slips resembled canals. As always they were clogged with vessels of all sizes and stations, from the lowly two-man

dinghys that gather harbor jetsam to the sleek
traders that bring amber from the north and
mammoth-ivory from the south.

The *Silver Gull* was a coastal ship with several
four-cornered sails captained by the youngest son
of an ambitious merchant. She lay in her own
slip, surrounded by shouting porters loading bales
of raw linen and quarrelsome sailors doing mys-
terious knots in the rigging. Seeing his patroness'
approach the captain hurried through the press
to help them aboard. "Princess, great lady, welcome back!" the fellow greeted her with oily
effusion. "Did your quest meet with good fortune? Ah, I see! Magi, many wizards to save
Mishbil! Lords, Magister, be pleased to step
aboard. Welcome to the *Silver Gull.* There is sore
need of your help!"

The deck-planks were wedged back in place
over the full hold. Zaryas had the only cabin, a
tiny wooden chamber on the aft deck that she
had to share with the stores. The magi were
allotted comfortable quarters under an awning
nearby. With infinite clatter and confusion,
shouted contradictory advice from the helpfully
inclined, both aship and ashore, and several halts
while checks for possibly forgotten items were
made, the *Silver Gull* wallowed out of the harbor,
towed by perhaps a dozen small rowboats. There
was a long pause while the lines were cast off
and coiled back up, and then with a surge and a
leap the ship slowly came alive. The yellow
glazed-linen sails tauntened and strained, a fresh
salty breeze swept away the harbor stenches,

and a curl of white foam fell away on either side where the keel cut through the bottle-green waves.

From where she clung to the rail Zaryas could see the Sun, modest behind a lemon-tinted haze, hanging straight before the high carven prow. Six leagues to the east the bay opened out, and there, with due care to miss the shoals and treacherous currents, the *Gull* could turn south and run down the coastline to Mishbil. A leisurely day and night asea should see her home again.

So long as they did not interfere with the sailors' work the passengers could go anywhere and, leaving his subordinates to unpack, the Master Magus made haste to indulge the usual magian curiosity. Zaryas went with him. "I've been thinking," she said. "How shall the magi force the land around Mishbil to sink again?"

"We can't," the Magus said absently. Sailors were aloft adjusting the smaller sails, while their captain bawled instructions from below. The Magus tested the wind's speed by holding out his long trailing red sleeve. "If the shore is really rising it is inexorable, the earth itself moving in her sleep—no more reversible than the winds."

"You herognomers can command the airs," Zaryas pointed out.

"Then I should say, no more reversible than the turning Sun above us," the Magus said. "The best we may hope for is swift accommodation to new conditions." Stepping carefully over a coil of rope the Magus fingered the intricate carving of the ladder-rail before ascending to the steering deck. "Most folk think magi coerce nature," he continued. "But the truth of it is we serve her, cajoling her along the path we want—as the captain steers his ship. Or rather, as the helmsman does," he added, since the captain was plainly busy interfering with someone else's work. "There are immutable rules that no persuasion will swerve, and the first and greatest of these is that all things, men and canals both, have an allotted time of usefulness. No physic will avail after that point."

Zaryas shivered. "That is my fear," she admitted. "That we attempt the impossible. Perhaps I ought to send my people elsewhere—select another townsite upstream."

This weakening of will was so unusual the Magus hastened to say, "Of course we haven't examined the parameters of the problem yet. There may be some quite simple solution that will rejuvenate the Dragon for eons to come."

"Mishbil seethes with hydromants," Zaryas said. "Unless they're all fools every simple solution has already been tried."

Of course the Magus could not admit this possibility. "I have absolute faith in the competence of our southern brethren," he said. "But new eyes may see new points."

The *Silver Gull* hugged the northern shore of the bay, for the southern is shallow and stony. The sheer gray crags to their left seemed almost close enough to touch, and Zaryas hoped the captain would not meddle with his helmsman. The lonely cry of cliff-nesting terns drifted to her ears mingled with the murmur of sea against stone. Close to the water-line the tide had worn an endless uncharted honeycomb of low caverns and fissures, perennial refuges for smugglers, murderers, and pirates. The Sun, having burnt off the morning mists, slanted past these hidey-holes and lent them an air of gloomy mystery. Zaryas could hear the hollow echo of waves lapping the secret parts of the rock.

Food, as Xantallon had complained, is a favorite interest in Averidan, where an ideal life is expressed as five meals a day. So when the *Gull* was well under way the captain ordered a small repast served under the deck awning. Strong yellow wine in globular glass bottles, elegant rolls of barley bread, sliced fruits soaked in brandy, tiny fish fried to a delicate brown—the captain had made an effort to impress and delight his high-ranked guests. "He's wasted asea," the Magus whispered to Zaryas. "He ought to keep a tavern."

When the platters were cleared away the magi dispersed to explore the ship. "Would my lady care for a round of Thumbprint?" the captain offered.

"Certainly." Zaryas smiled. "The millennium-old game is a favorite all Averidan over. The 144 ceramic tiles made a cheerful clatter when Zaryas shook them in their bag. Soon bets were laid and the trestle table webbed with interlocking rows of six-sided tiles.

When Zaryas jumped three Green birds and so reversed them into two Pears and a Cat's-Eye she won. The captain counted out his losses and pouted, "You're a cunning hand at it, my lady."

Though it was no pleasure to gamble with a bad loser, Zaryas offered, saying, "Let me give you an opportunity to win these back."

Before noon the *Gull* came to open sea. The turn south was accomplished without incident. As the afternoon wore away the wind began to drop, blowing in fitful and contrary gusts that forced the unfortunate sailors to scramble up and down the rigging. Off the starboard rail Zaryas could look west to the shore. For lack of water that part of Averidan is nearly unpeopled. The only mark of man was a fisherman's lonely shanty in a narrow cove. Beyond rolled desolate ocher ridges of sandy rock and sterile thornthickets. Heat lay almost visibly over all, shimmering in the distance, thickening the air until it looked like water. On the hazy horizon far to the north a smear of thin yellow cloud menaced the desert.

"Sandstorm," said the captain, pointing it out to Zaryas. "But it won't blow our way." He shook the bag and held it out for her to choose tiles for another round. But Zaryas shook her head. It would be unmannerly to beggar her host.

Unfortunately the cloud roiled closer as the *Silver Gull* dawdled. "Come on, you lazy thing," Zaryas urged the ship. "Move!" The *Gull* tacked back and forth before the wayward breeze, unhearing. It was as if the sea water had transmogrified into glue, dragging at the ship until its doom could catch up. Neither Zaryas' impatience,

nor the captain's frenzied orders, nor even the
Master Magus' herognomical breezes would master the *Gull*. With the suddenness of nightfall
the airborne sand loomed mountain-high over the
shore, blotting out the afternoon sunshine. The
now-chilly breeze plucked at Zaryas' tunic, and
she realized their peril. Such storms kill not only
with battering wind but with blinding sands.
She mentioned her fears to the captain.

"It's nothing, it'll pass over," he assured her.
Even as he spoke sail and wave hung slack for a
moment, cowering against the anger to come. Then
with a howl of fury the tempest swept in.

Fine choking grit raged round them. Like a
scalded cat the *Gull* leaped forward, propelled
up and down invisible swells at terrifying speed.
Yet to her blinded passengers she seemed to also
spin sickeningly in one place, determined to dive
for cover under the waves. Within the space of a
breath Zaryas could not see an arm's length before her. The stinging sand tore at her face. Her
straw traveling hat was whipped away, and her
loosened black braids seemed to be plucking themselves right off her head. Shielding eyes and
mouth in her sleeve Zaryas stumbled along the
deck, groping at each step lest she fall overboard.
The roar of furious wind and tormented sea con-
fused her, and with a dazing crack of bone she
bumped her head against someone. It was the
captain, who bellowed, "All we can do is run
before it, princess! This can't last long!"

"Idiot!" Zaryas exclaimed, but the wind tore
her words away. Demonic voices shrieked in her

ears, malicious phantom hands dragged the *Gull*
along. There was no opportunity to cut the sails
loose, and the storm wrenched them and their
masts every which way. Deep in the hold of the
Gull the timbers moaned as the masts twisted in
their sockets. The keel was being levered apart.

But as the Magus said, all things have their
allotted span. Though the wind did not drop the
blinding sands whirled themselves farther out to
sea. Everyone gasped in the suddenly clear air,
spat out grit, and rubbed their eyes. The mutter
of hungry water as it seeped into the innards of
the ship was the only sound for a moment. Then
the sailors howled for Ennelith's mercy, the captain burst into tears, and Zaryas' maids screamed to Viris and their mistress. The Master Magus quickly dominated the uproar. "None shall
drown!" he announced. "To the buckets! We must
bail for it!"

The passengers shrank back out of the way.
The sailors raced to rip out the deck planks while
others tumbled down the ladders into the hold
with buckets. On both sides bucketsful of water
flew up and out. But with dismay Zaryas saw
the bilge slowly rising past the bundles of cargo,
despite their efforts.

"We can help too." The Magus nodded to his
hydromants. Three thick-glass wands drew out
lumps of water from the hold—beads, fruits,
globes of clear, jelly-quivering water. Magically
they were coaxed up and over the rail into the
sea. The Magus caught Zaryas' eye. "Just in
case—"

She nodded. "We'll hedge our bets." Quietly she drew her three aides aft. There was room in the cabin for them if the door stood ajar. She began unhooking sausages from their ceiling hooks. "We must be cast up ashore without provisions," she said to them. She could feel the shift and sag of the deck under her feet as she hurried to the *Gull*'s dinghy. It was lashed upside-down to the deck near the portside rail. Xerlanthor helped her to cut the lines and turn the boat over. When she looked over the rail she was shocked to see how far away the shore was. The storm had pushed the *Gull* far out to sea.

Following her example her staff ran back and forth, packing provisions and supplies with feverish haste into the boat. "Food and water-jugs first," she directed. "And don't forget to leave room for someone to row the boat." A thought came to her, and she went back to the cabin. From her luggage she took out her only weapon, a short bronze sword, and tied it to her back. She thanked Viris the Foremother she wore sensible traveling clothes, red leather buskins and loose linen trousers under a short robe, for there was no time to change. She rolled a blanket around the bag of Thumbprint tiles; they were enameled and too expensive to lose. "Magister," she called, "is there anything in your bundles irreplaceable?"

But when the storm struck the magi had instinctively hugged their mirrors, the badge and chief tool (with their staffs) of the Order. Each round covered glass was already safe, hooked to belts or tucked into pouches. "Good," the Magus approved. He turned courteously to the captain. "Shall we launch the boat now?"

"The boat, yes!" The distracted captain started at the idea. "Ladies, to the boat! Oh, Ennelith Sea-Queen, what shall I do without my beautiful *Silver Gull*?"

"Cease your moaning, man!" Zaryas snapped. "You, sailor, go lower the boat—"

But it was too late. With a sickening wallow the ship sank lower yet, listing more and more to the starboard. The shock made everyone stagger. The hold filled quickly now. The sailors had to stop bailing and scramble up to the deck. Without any sense of having lost a battle or turned a corner, Zaryas realized they were all clinging to a wreck. The *Gull* would not actually sink out of sight. Her wide wooden hull had some innate buoyancy, and by great good fortune the cargo was linens and spice—bulky yet light—rather than ingots or pottery which would drag her down. But the passengers might not live to enjoy the *Gull*'s final equilibrium.

The deck slanted so that it was impossible to stand anymore. Passengers and crew alike clung to the rails, masts or ropes. The dinghy, still hitched to the port rail, hung now high out of reach. "And it's too far to swim," the captain moaned. "We're all going to drown."

Only the magi were calm. "If only the wind would drop," the Magus told them cheerfully. "we could lift you all to shore."

"Try anyway, wind or no," Zaryas urged. "The *Gull* was settling so quickly the water crept over the starboard rails. She tried to dig her finger-nails into the oak boards and lever herself a little higher.

The Magus frowned as the wavelets wet his shoes, and he shook his feet like a cat. Precariously, he levered himself upright on the slippery deck and tested the wind. "Let us try," he told his subordinates. "Xerlanthor?"

The young magus unwound himself from his perch on a spar. Without ceremony he grasped a sailor by one arm and rose slowly straight up. Those watching held their breath as feet parted company with deck and the two hung unsupported in mid-air. The gusts freshened around and beneath them. All magi study herognomy enough to walk the winds, just as they all dabble enough in hydromancy to scry. But to lift the weight of another person is just barely within their power. The hems and wide sleeves of Xerlanthor's red robe snapped in the brisk wind, absurdly resembling butterfly wings. He rose higher, narrowly missed tangling his burden in some ropes, and deposited the sailor in the dinghy. "Not too bad," he reported. "But we can't get everyone into this boat."

"We'll have to risk lifting farther, then," the Magus said. At his nod Xantallon hoisted an ashen-faced aide up. The two soared high above the masts before drifting shoreward. Everyone watched anxiously until like a buzzard in borrowed plumes the red-clad figure dropped. Zaryas

saw the distant splash as the aide tumbled off
into the surf. Freed from the weight Xantallon
rebounded upward and began floating back.

"We'll do it yet," Zaryas said. "The magi will
lift your men up to the boat," she told the captain. "You can lower it and row to shore while
the magi ferry everyone else there directly." Nervously she wondered which was safer, flying with
magi or boating with a jinxed captain. But she
kept a calm countenance so that no one should
lose heart.

"Your turn now, my lady." Xerlanthor bowed
smiling before her. Before Zaryas could argue he
caught her up lightly in his arms. Her stomach
seemed to plummet as the ship dropped away
and back. The wind no longer tugged at her, for
now she rode in it as fish ride the waves in their
element. Hastily she turned her attention from
the churning sea below.

"Is my sword in your way?"

"No." His brow was furrowed with concentration as they rose, but when they leveled off and
began to soar toward land he relaxed a bit. "Isn't
it a little melodramatic?"

"In the desert no one meets a friend," she
quoted the old proverb.

"I don't wager, but you tempt me," he smiled.

"You don't?" Most Veridese will happily bet
on either side of any question whatever. "Why
not?"

"I always win," he said blandly. "And haven't
we had our allotment of incident this trip?"

It was a challenge. Zarays' pointed face, bur-

nished by Sun and wind, further sharpened with
glee until she seemed to scintillate like a cut
topaz. "What will you stake?"

He glanced away from her. "The traditional
stake in bets between young folk is a seashell."

He was so near she could smell the faint harsh-
ness of new red dye in his magus robe. Seashells
are exchangeable for one kiss all Averidan over.
Zaryas could not define her feelings, supported
as she was between earth and sky by his power
alone, and so said nothing. Yet she felt impelled
to reply. When they sailed low over the tidal
flats she exclaimed, "It's a bet, then!" and wriggled free. Xerlanthor yelped in dismay as she fell
a little more than her own height to the damp
sands, landing on her feet agile as a cat. Her
maids ran to her aid, while magi swooped in to
investigate, the sound of their scolding swept
toward them by the wind.

The laden dinghy was lowered and slowly
pulled away from the hapless *Gull*. Sailors clung
to its sides or paddled behind. Even over the
roar of the surf the wail of the captain's voice
could be heard, mourning his loss. Zaryas quickly
organized the castaways lest the mismanaged boat
founder. But though no oar dipped into the sea
in time with another the landfall was at last
achieved without mishap.

"We must make camp," Zaryas commanded.
"Mishbil isn't far. We can walk there tomorrow—
cut inland to the main south road. I suppose,"
she asked the Magus, "there's no spring hereabouts?"

The Magus passed the question to Xantallon and the other two hydromants. After lengthy consultation, pointing in every direction with their thick glass wands, they confirmed Zaryas' pessimism. "Any source would have someone living near it," Xantallon said. "Water is the blood of the desert."

"A very Mishbil-like saying," Zaryas agreed. "We'll just have to be sparing of our flasks."

Xerlanthor and the geomants selected a camp site, not searching for geomantic currents of luck or stability but merely choosing a cozy nook between two sand dunes sheltered from the prevailing wind. As the Sun, now low in the west, dyed the dunes a glorious sanguine hue, a campfire of driftwood was lit. The sullen pounding surf did not quite disguise the silence pressing down around them, a silence of empty yet secretive desert, ever more watchful as night crept in from the sea. Everyone was glad to gather together, relax, and talk over the day's terrors. A flask of the expensive golden wine was opened—though there were not enough cups—and a frugal meal of ship-bread and sausage prepared.

Xerlanthor bent near Zaryas' ear as he refilled her mug. "You could have hurt yourself, jumping down like that," he said in a low voice. "Do I have so untrustworthy a manner?"

"Not at all," she replied, smiling up at him. But there was no opportunity to say more. She was secretly glad of it. Zaryas had left the selection of a mate to time and chance, being too busy governing Mishbil to sort the genuine suitors from the merely ambitious. Instinctively now she felt that time was her ally. There was as yet no hurry, no heat of blood pulsing to fruition.

Chapter 3: 3 Arbas

They slept round the embers of the fire, snuggled together like tired puppies. Though the day's scorching heat lingered in the sands for a long time, by dawn the desert's cold had roused everyone. Zaryas tucked her chilly hands into her armpits and shivered under the thin quilt. A watery yellow streak where the sea met the sky heralded the new day. As the fire was poked back to life the sailors came up to her and nudged a spokesman forward.

"We'd rather not walk to Mishbil, my lady," the man told her. "Sailors are happiest asea. Rowing the boat down the coast we could get home near as soon as you."

"What does your captain say to this?" she asked.

"You can have him," the seaman returned sourly. "He's bad luck, a born land-lubber."

So with their share of the provisions the crew of the lost *Silver Gull* pushed off. Their miserable captain, head in hands, still bemoaned his loss and would not look up to see the departure.

"We also must go, and soon," Zaryas said. "Let's get as far as we can before the heat of the day descends. It'll be warmer walking anyway."

The brisk air and tentative light suggested cool dew as its natural attendant. But each breath Zaryas drew was clean and dry as laundry fresh from the clothesline. As they walked west the golden light behind them increased, throwing long moving blue shadows up and over the dunes. The arching sky ahead grew wan and purple, then very slowly blue, the deep yet hot blue of thistle-blossoms. Day had arrived.

Once the shore had been left behind, the country was the same in every direction as far as Zaryas could see—lifeless ocher sandstone ridges and sandy ocher valleys in which only thorn shrubs eked out a sparse existence. The very sight induced thirst. Zaryas made a quick count—there were eleven magi, her two maids and three aides. Counting herself and the captain there were eighteen to share the contents of their four pottery watercasks: sufficient, with care. The casks were as big as her torso, not at all convenient for transport. They had to be carried suspended on a pole between two bearers. At midmorning pause to rest and shake sand out of their shoes, no one got more than a few sips.

It was weary work, trudging up and down the pathless hills. The stony ridges made Zaryas' feet sore. In the stuffy valleys the sand slid underfoot, adding to the labor of each stride, and the thorn-briers caught at them. As the Sun mounted, his warmth drew sticky spice-odors

from the bushes. When she snagged her sleeve on
the thorns the sap smelled sweet as perfume, yet
clung to her fingers like mucus.

However, by late morning the chief torment
had become the heat. The Sun was hotter than
molten brass in the sky, beating on foreheads and
shoulders, weighting feet like manacles. In the
valleys where there was a little shade the air was
hot and unmoving. The Sun heated the ridges
until the stone seemed to scorch right through
boot-soles. Bitterly regretting the loss of her hat,
Zaryas wiped dust and sweat from her brow and
shielded it under a fold of cloak.

The road, when they reached it, was a disap-
pointment. Insensibly Zaryas had begun to think
of it as it is near the City—a wide thoroughfare
paved with oyster shell and lime, lined with
trees, bustling with merchants and vendors. But
all she saw when they topped a ridge before noon
was a narrow trail, the lime so mingled with
drifted sand the road was yellow too. Weathered
round stones painted with the green emblem of
the Shan King marked the way at infrequent
intervals. There was nobody on it, north or south,
as far as they could see.

"No one of sense walks to Mishbil in the summer," Zaryas admitted. "But I did hope we'd see
somebody."

"At least the going will be easier now," Xerlanthor replied.

In a breathlessly stuffy little ravine they settled down to rest until the grilling noon heat
should pass. It was difficult to fall asleep in such

discomfort, but Zaryas was tired enough to drop off at last.

As soon as the edge was taken off her weariness, however, the heat woke her again. Her loose white linen robe was damp with sweat. Zaryas rose, loosening her sash and shaking out her sleeves to draw cooler air next to the skin. Everyone else was rather restlessly asleep as she stepped quietly away from her place.

The Sun had declined a little from his zenith, but his power still smote on her bare head like a hammer. She was unstoppering a water cask when a few grains of coarse sand fell with a tinkling noise onto it. She looked up. On the little ledge above crouched a lithe dappled form, so nearly the yellow of the rock that only the long writhing tail showed clearly: a sand leopard.

"Wake!" She whirled and gave shrill warning. "Leopards!" Her cry echoed eerily off the rocky walls, and everyone started up blinking and gabbling questions. Sand leopards favor surprise attacks. If their victims panic and run, the great cats can easily chase down their prey. For a moment the tactic seemed effective. Recognizing the alarm four leopards charged down in a flurry of sand. The nearest beast leaped right over Zaryas' head to land near the captain, slashing out with both daggered front paws.

Like a fool the man burrowed under his cloak, screaming, "Help! Save me!"

"Curse you for a complete idiot!" Xerlanthor swore. He snatched up the cloak and flung it at the charging leopard, then while the beast dodged

raised his wand. The arm-length rod was ground
out of the usual black stone, reinforced at intervals with bronze bands. With a gesture from it
Xerlanthor geomantically raised a blinding puff of
yellow sand. The captain scrambled away while
Zaryas unsheathed her sword and dashed in to
chop at the engulfing cloud. "Don't do that, it's
dangerous," Xerlanthor ordered, but she quar-
tered the magically roiled sands until her wide
slicing blade returned red.

A howl of enraged pain emerged and the cloud
blundered over the scattered luggage leaving a
trail of gory blots. In a series of messy blind
blows Zaryas disabled the creature. Then Xerlanthor dropped his geomancy and surveyed the
writhing leopard with distaste. "Not tidy," he
complained. "And what a waste, look what you've
done to the pelt."

Chopping the beast's throat through Zaryas
snapped, "We won. That's all that matters."

Two herognomers had quickly captured another leopard by jointly lifting it, howling, high
off the ground. When it became plain their prey
intended to make a fight of it the other leopards
fled. "Let's take this one to Mishbil and tame it,"
Xerlanthor proposed.

The Master Magus looked up at the captive
leopard, suspended almost three times man-height
above them. "A cub you might manage," he said,
"but a full-grown beast is impossible."

"These cats are a pest and menace," Zaryas
added her objection.

"I suppose we must be practical," the Magus

decided, and with a swift downward gesture of herognomical fans the leopard was dashed to its death on the rocks. The younger magi cut up and examined the anatomy of the carcass with happy interest, while Zaryas and the Magus agreed that after this excitement some food would soothe everyone's raveled nerves.

"And we might as well carry the provisions inside us as on our backs," Zaryas said. So with one thing and another they did not start south again until well after noon.

It was almost a relief to take the road again. With a sigh Zaryas relaxed into a long steady stride, looking forward to taking up her work at home. Would Norveth her deputy have inspected each of the ordered dredgers and earth-haulers for signs of shoddy workmanship or deceptive practice before handing over the money to the Metalworkers? She doubted it. Had that questionable boatload of barley been accepted by the mutinous grain merchant, or had he spitefully left the sacks neglected on the docks till the musty grain sprouted in the bag? Like most folk with the gift of efficiency Zaryas never believed anything could run properly without her hand on the helm. She did not quite expect Mishbil to have collapsed in her four-day absence, but she would not be surprised if it had.

Instinctively she had taken up a position at the rear of the party—a good post for supervising the progress of everyone else. With a start she noticed the back her eye had been unaccountably fixed on, solid and red-clad and ever so slightly plump.

Picking up her pace, Zaryas caught up with the Master Magus and startled him very much by tucking his plump arm under her own. "Xarlim, may I ask your personal advice?"

The Magus hastily adjusted his red cap. With the justified pride of an elderly hen setting twelve eggs he said, "I would be honored, my dear lady, to lend you the wisdom of my years. Our counsel on private matters is rarely asked, but we magi are widely learned."

"Xerlanthor lost a wager to me," she began.

"Ah! and can't pay up?" The Magus smiled but shook his head. "The scamp, playing Thumbprint with wealthy women. He's intelligent, a gifted geomant, but sometimes I wonder about his temperament. Don't let him off, it will be a lesson to him." Then, catching a sidewise glimpse of Zaryas' smile, he demanded, "What was the stake?"

"A seashell," she told him, and choked with laughter at his expression.

"The presumptuous— That's just not done!" the Magus sputtered. "Only a life of moderation allows a magi a proper devotion to their work."

"You mean, to escape the distractions of family life," cynical Zaryas said. "Of course most magi are too busy to wed. But not all of you, all the time—that wouldn't be moderation."

"True," the Magus admitted. "After all, our most important concern is magery. It's better to marry—"

"Or *not* marry," Zaryas put in.

"Or not marry," the Magus conceded unhappily. "It's considered better to relieve drives rather than let them become a distraction, and perhaps fuddle your thinking."

"That's what I thought the custom was," Zaryas said with satisfaction.

"But there's more to this than just what custom allows!" the Magus exclaimed. "The difference in rank—and he's in your service too, as we all are! How far has this progressed?"

"Only as far as a wager," Zaryas assured him.

"You must erase the debt immediately," the Magus said.

"I don't see how," Zaryas said in her most blandly unhelpful tone. "Suppose I set up a bet to lose and then win anyway? I'm notoriously lucky. Then he would owe me two."

The Magus stared at her. "You really intend to pursue this?"

Zaryas denied it. "I haven't lost my heart at all. I merely intend to keep my choices open. The situation interests me. After all, I've never been wooed by a magus before. But I'll follow your advice—not to let him off—to the letter."

"You little hellcat," the Magus moaned.

So unchanging were the rolling yellow sand-hills that it was difficult to believe walking really made any difference. The glowing Sun reddened as the afternoon waned. At last, when it was a great flattened ruby sphere on the horizon, they topped the final ridge and saw the city of Mishbil spread in the valley below, purple and gold in the westering light. It sprawled comfortably spiderlike between the fields and the sea. Where the capital is all up and down, the simplicity of cliffs falling into laughing sea, wide Mishbil has the flat reserve of a locked gate. Her secret places are not high and lofty, open only to sky, but squirreled in mazes of stone and water, plain to see yet impossible to come to.

The younger magi were not too weary to raise a cheer. The promise of rest, of food, and above all of water—water to drink, to cool tired feet, to wash off the dust of travel, water that is the blood of Mishbil-in-the-desert—all these thoughts lent speed to their descent.

The broad valley was netted like the skin of a cantaloupe with canals. "See the Dragon—" Zaryas pointed. "Mishbil is the head, with the chin resting on the seashore, and the Bilcad is the curving spine."

"And the bluffs are its wings," the Magus added. From their vantage-point the reptile was plain to see, scaled in a patchwork of fields, collared like a proper Viridese dragon with a great lacy ruff of canal-trenches, and winking with one glittering green eye—the lily-pond in the center of town.

The road wound steeply down into the valley and then arched over a canal. There Zaryas had to wait, for in their zeal the magi insisted on clambering down the embankment to examine this first water-channel.

As she had told them, the canals were dry. When Xantallon scuffed away the thick green scum at the bottom he uncovered only crusted silt that rose in powdery clouds. The successive dry lines left by the diminishing waters were duly measured and noted on waxen tablets. Only Xerlanthor stood aloof on the embankment.

"Aren't you going down to examine the local earth currents?" Zaryas asked him.

He stared southwest across the wide Bilcad valley and did not reply at first. Since the river had worn a deep channel for itself it could not be seen. The desert was reclaiming its own. The fields, usually so startlingly green against the sands, were sterile. Here and there a stubborn farmer had sown seed anyway, defiantly gambling on a once-a-lifetime rain. Those plots bore a mournful stubble of yellow seedlings, dry and sparse as the pelt of a mangy dog. "Will your folk really starve?" he asked.

"Not this year," she replied in a low voice. The speculation was almost physically painful, like a toothache. She probed the tender spot warily. "The barley stored against famine could last the winter, with care. And after that—" She pressed her lips tightly together. "I could always petition the Shan King for a few more boatloads. But without more water sooner or later. . . ."

"It's not a question of *more* water," he said pettishly. "It's getting what water there is up to where the canals are."

"Of course we could have the whole system redug," Zaryas said. "It would only take a generation or two, after all."

He smiled. "Let's not quarrel," he said. "Have you ever examined the canals of the western Mhesan River?"

"No."

"Little earthen dikes held in place by geomancy stick out into the river and direct water into the canals."

"That would do no good here," she pointed out.

"It might if we built the dike right across the river channel—a dam, as it were."

"Dam the Bilcad?" The idea was startling. "How could anyone leash the Dragon?"

"Such dams have been built before," Xerlanthor said. "On a smaller scale—streams or mountain creeks, mostly. This would be the largest ever attempted. But it might well be possible."

Zaryas discovered she did not dare believe him. "Would that raise the water level to where it used to be?" she demanded. "Everything would be the same as it was? We wouldn't have to dig new canals?"

"You'd lose some tillage at first," Xerlanthor warned. "A lake would form behind the dam. And shipping on the Bilcad would be disrupted. But old canals could be extended later, new lands reclaimed from the desert.

Below, the dusty magi were climbing back up to the road, pausing only to argue and draw little diagrams. Xerlanthor said, "Don't discuss this idea with anyone yet, if you don't mind. It wouldn't do to raise false hopes."

"Rat," Zaryas accused. "What about *my* hopes?" All of a sudden, tired as she was, she could have danced in the dusty road for joy. The surge of crazy hope, even the distant prospect of salvation, was more intoxicating than plum brandy on an empty stomach. With a whoop of excitement she threw her arms around his shoulders. Xerlanthor staggered back but did not quite fall over. The puffing Master Magus hauled his bulk over the verge and glared at them, his mouth pursed in disapproval.

Chapter 4: The Rest of Arbas

In Averidan the etiquette of hospitality is ossi-
fied in tradition. After the rigors and unexpected
perils of the southward journey it was expected
by all that barring sudden emergency no business would be so much as thought of for at least
a week. Even Zaryas did not dare initiate serious
discussions until her guests were fully rested.

Since the shipment of tools had indeed been
defective she had a ready outlet for surplus energies at hand. By the time Norveth had been suit-
ably scolded, the many flaws in the tools pointed
out to the metalworkers, and a promise of resti-
tution extracted—and by the time all the work
accumulated in her absence had been dealt with—
five days had passed.

Arguing to herself that the magnitude of Mishbil's peril demanded haste, on the sixth day at
the earliest allowable hour Zaryas sent for the
magi. The prospect of waiting politely for her
guests in the hall was intolerable. Instead she
prowled fretfully through the courtyard and gar-

den of the rambling old city mansion in which every viceroy had lived and worked. In Mishbil where water is life even the humblest home has its lily basin or shallow reflecting pool. Despite the agricultural drought no one had yet had to give up this luxury—the city lay well downstream. The viceroy's columned courtyard was particularly graceful, with a tinkling fountain in an oval pool surrounded by dozens of wide pottery basins glazed white and blazing with water lilies, red and gold and white. Mint grew beside the waters and climbing vines on the walls. But the music of the water grated on Zaryas' ear, and the perfume of the lilies was oppressive. To perceive a task yet not be able to set hand to it was maddening.

The old gardener-woman grumbled when Zaryas began minutely inspecting the lily-pots for signs of slipshod care. At last the old woman set down her trowel and remarked, "He'll arrive in good time, my lady, so you needn't poke up the silt like that."

"I'm checking for water-mites," Zaryas said, and then demanded, "Who will arrive?"

"The wizard-lad you have your eye on," the old woman said in a severe tone. "Of course you ought to wed and settle down, but no good comes of meddling with magi."

Rumor has a life in Averidan independent of fact, a Viridese weakness Zaryas had often used to advantage. But now she could not suppress a gasp of surprise. "You wicked old harridan!" she exclaimed. "Where ever did you hear that?"

"It's in the plaiv," the other replied. "All the stories say magi work too much with their heads to use their pricks much."

Zaryas could have screamed with impatience. Keeping one ear open for approaching footsteps she said, "No, no, I mean about *me*. And—" But after all Xerlanthor's name stuck in her throat.

"Common knowledge," the old woman informed her. "Do you know what else I heard yesterday? It seems we don't need hydromants to redig the canals after all. The Dragon only wants propitiation, to get the water to flow properly again."

This new idea diverted Zaryas' rage. "What kind of offering would please it?" she asked. "I brought spices up to the Sun Temple."

"Haven't an idea," the old gardener muttered. She tucked her gardening tools into a tattered basket and suggested, "Money, perhaps?"

Taking this for a hint, Zaryas discreetly laid a few coppers on the stone coping of the fountain. "And I'm not in the least interested in any of the magi," she lied. "If you must gossip, gossip truly."

With a sketchy salute of farewell the old woman pocketed the coins and shuffled away—not, to Zaryas' annoyance, quite swiftly enough, for the magi were just arriving. Xerlanthor blinked when the old woman gave him a malicious wrinkled grin that revealed three yellow teeth. To distract him Zaryas announced, "I've just learned a new theory to account for our water problem," and recounted the propitiation idea."

"Superstition," the Master Magus snorted. "Just

because the Bilcad looks like a dragon doesn't mean it really is one."

"How do you know?" Zaryas asked. "It sounds reasonable."

Xantallon yawned prodigiously. "You routed us out so early to discuss that?"

"No," Zaryas said. All her frustrations and bad temper came bubbling back. "You've rested enough, all of you. Get to work!"

The magi took this abrupt command in good spirit. Quickly the work was divided by the Master Magus. The hydromants were set to examining the methods of their local brethren in calculating canal capacity. Herognomers double-checked statistics on evaporation from both channel and field. And with the enthusiasm of hungry puppies the geomants measured the entire canal complex's height above sea level.

To Zaryas' surprise Xerlanthor did not mention his proposal as magian consensus hardened. By the end of the month the Master Magus was ready to make a formal report to Zaryas and the Council of Mishbil.

The Council was a quarrelsome body of fifty responsible elders, guildmasters, priestesses, landowners, and magi. They met for coolness' sake on the marble terrace of Zaryas' house. This wide platform was nearly as private as the hall, since it overlooked the Eye Pool. Passersby could look over across the Pool, now heady with the perfume of white and yellow water lilies, but could hear nothing.

Zaryas was splendid in her official robes of

thick white silk barred at sleeve, shoulder and
hem with deep green. Wide sleeves lined with
green brocade embroidered with gold flower-and-
shell motifs fell from her shoulders into a lus-
trous crumpled heap on either side of her chair.
Beside her sat the Mistress of the Sodality of
Ennelith, in sapphire satins. As representative
of the Sea Goddess, the Mistress ranked second
only to Zaryas. But she would have sat near
anyway; the Mistress was by far the most sensible member of the Council. To do the occasion
honor the other Council members had also donned
their most vivid formal robes. Ruby and gold and
amethyst and turquoise, only the deep emerald-
green of Shan royalty was missing. Zaryas fan-
cied that the Dragon's eye must be aglitter with
the colorful brilliance, as if an unfallen tear trembled in the strong morning light on its imaginary
eyelashes.

One by one the visiting magi were presented
to the Council. Zaryas noticed one or two second
glances when Xerlanthor was introduced. Several shallow map-trays, big as tabletops, were
laid on the pavement at their feet, and the Master Magus pointed to the first with his fan. "This
first tray is twenty-five generations old, and rep-
resents the Bilcad and its canals as they were at
that time."

Zaryas rose to examine it. Wax had been molded
over a clay foundation to form a minute but exact landscape. Contours—"measured distances
above sea level," the Magus told them—were
marked by red thread pinned to the dusty wax,

and the waxen lining of the network of canals was tinted blue. "You may see how beautifully it was designed," the Magus said, signaling to the servants again. They brought him a large glass pitcher of water and, with his assistants' help, the Magus poured a thin steady stream of water into the miniature Bilcad. The water flowed down the waxen river valley to the baked-clay sea, filling the canals on its way. Unfortunately over the years the seams of the "sea" had warped and cracked with age. The water leaked out onto the pavement to wet Zaryas' shoes. But the effect was impressive all the same.

"This second tray," the Magus said, "is our work. We've followed the color conventions of our predecessors, so that you may see changes clearly."

The modern work, cobbled together so hastily, was much less fine. Unmolded wax was heaped on the edges, and rough fired-clay edges snagged silken sleeves. As Zaryas bent over it she was struck by how deeply the Bilcad's channel was cut. "But you can see," the Magus told her, "that it's not the river sinking, but the land rising. Look at the sea-level contours." And indeed each red thread had crept closer to the sea over the ages.

"Now see," the Magus said, and lifted the pitcher again. The water ran down the modeled river as before, but no longer rose high enough to fill many of the canals. Other canals conducted water for only a fraction of their length.

"That's exactly how the water ran last season

at home," the matriarch of the largest barley farm exclaimed, pointing. "Look, how clever, they even have the little extra canal-intake my sons dug last year."

"It didn't help, did it," Xerlanthor said, and she had to own it hadn't.

"Year by year as the river cut lower," the Magus said, "the canal mouths were redug, farther and farther upstream, to reach water. This last push, extending the canals west past those little bluffs, must have taken a generation to excavate."

The last tray held a representation of the proposed revamped system. "As you can see," the Magus said, "the existing canals are dug much deeper, reshaped, and lined with dressed stone to facilitate the flow of water. We'll blast away these outcrops of bedrock, and straighten the channels." He demonstrated, and indeed the water flowed properly.

"But the labor for all this will be incredible," Zaryas protested. "Look how deep those canals are. What will we eat while all this work is done? And think of the cost! What guarantee will we have that these canals also won't be rendered useless over time?"

"None whatsoever," the Magus said bluntly. "I warned you, you know. Nothing lasts forever."

"I've laid out a fifty-year schedule of construction," Xantallon said, "and a rough estimate of costs."

Zaryas and the Council examined the figures with horror. "It will take all our surplus revenue, and more," Zaryas complained. "And for fifty years! Who knows the future? Suppose a crop fails, or sickness strikes, or the Shan King declares war on somebody? On so narrow a margin we'd all starve!"

"It's the only solution," the Magus solemnly told the Council, and the other magi nodded agreement.

And then Xerlanthor stepped forward smiling. "No, it isn't," he said. "I've thought of another." His clear voice carried to every ear.

Before the Master Magus could interrupt, Zaryas cut in. "Tell us more of this," she commanded grandly.

Xerlanthor bowed deeply before her, only the barest wry twist of his mouth betraying amusement. "I can show you, my lady," he said. Plucking some of the excess wax from the second tray he warmed and shaped it in his hands. Fascinated, Zaryas watched the strong clever fingers flex and work, long and cunning and deft as a potter's. "My plan involves blocking the Bilcad to force the water up. See here on the landscape as it is now, just below the lowest canal mouth." He forced the roll of softened wax into the model river channel and pinched it up into a little humped curve like a bent finger. "We'll dam the river completely. These outcrops of rock here can help anchor the ends of the construction. Now, the water."

At Xerlanthor's commanding gesture the servants gave him the pitcher. The water ran downstream but backed up at the waxen dam to form a pool that crept up until it flooded and filled every canal. "Spillways would then let the extra water run downstream," Xerlanthor explained. "A dam would be no less labor than canals. More, in fact, since all the work must be done in one season, between floods. But it's a permanent solution, good no matter how high the land ever rises."

Everyone spoke at once, acclaiming, rebuking, arguing. The Shan are an ancient race, secure enough in their ancestral unity to relish the acerbic pleasures of disagreement. The Master Magus fairly pounced on Xerlanthor, scolding, "And why didn't you confide this idea to me, your Master?" An elderly landowner whose property would become largely subaqueous huffed loudly about the virtues of traditional methods. The Master Metalworker offered the city a special bulk discount on shovels and stone-cutting tools.

In the middle of all this furor Zaryas was silent, knowing the ultimate decision, the final responsibility, was hers alone. Nothing, not her initial enthusiasm for a dam, nor even Xerlanthor's charm, could swerve her from the awful necessity of making the right decision. Her Council's shrill clamor rasped at her nerves. Being viceroy and princess had been strenuous but fun. She had not bargained for this terrifying burden, this decision on which Mishbil and all her people's future depended. It was as if she had been playing Thumbprint all this time with counters, and now had to bet her life. Suddenly her formal robes became a net, the splendor of the terrace and its view a cage. She leaped to her feet and clapped her hands for attention. "I shall seclude myself to consider the problem carefully," she announced, "and decide in three days. I may summon some of you and ask opinions, but in the meantime keep these proceedings to yourselves."

Even as she said this Zaryas knew it was futile. Every resident of Mishbil would know of the options by noon; at supper even the remote farmsteads would be debating the merits of dam versus canals. The news was too heady to let cool with standing.

With a perfunctory bow to the assembly she hurried indoors. The mansion was in the usual Viridese style, a secretive windowless street facade pierced by double gates opening into the inner garden. This outermost section housed the actual business of running Mishbil. Beyond the oval fountain and colonnaded garden, however, was another facade, another garden guarded by another gate. Zaryas sped through this inner gate, her wide ornate sleeves caught awkwardly over one arm, and warned the doorkeeper, "A great many people will try to see me the next few days. But no one is to enter except by my invitation."

The doorkeeper bowed. "Does that include the magi also, princess?"

"Of course not, they're the city's guests." She glanced at the guest wing, on the right, but its tall southeasterly windows reflected the strong sunshine so that nothing could be seen.

She turned to her own side and banged the door.

The chambers of the viceroy of Mishbil had once been the old servants' quarters, with little to recommend them but their cool northern exposure. However the last viceroy but two had been a builder of means, who had demanded and partially paid for a new wing. So now Zaryas trod on sparkling blue mosaic floors through high spacious rooms that held coolness like rare wine in polished agate cups.

She napped, as everyone in Mishbil does, through the noon heat. In the afternoon she watched through her shutter as farmers, merchants, dignitaries, and priestesses came through the first gates, round the fountain and down the walk, only to be turned away at the inmost gate. As she had thought, everybody with an interest hoped to influence the viceroy's decision. At last a stout red-clad figure approached and entered. Zaryas told her maid, "Go invite the Master Magus to sup with me."

She greeted him at a round table already spread with the delicacies of the city—fruit glazed with crystalline honey, icy mussels sprinkled with herbs, cold pigeon pie, pan-fried barley-flour cakes flavored with onion. As custom demanded, nothing serious was discussed during the meal.

At last the Magus set down his bowl. "Mishbil's cookery might put a serious dent in magian moderation," he said. "I've eaten more at a meal here than in two at home."

"Meat has more savor for the guest," Zaryas replied, quoting the proverb. She refilled their cups and carefully nestled the wine flask back into its bowl of chipped ice. "So, now—what do you think of the idea?"

"Xerlanthor's you mean?" The Magus sighed and swirled the deep red wine around in his cup. "Sometimes the lad is too subtle for my understanding. Secretive, insecure, ambitious—so—" The Magus groped for the word. "—so unmaguslike. When was the last time you saw an ambitious magus? Why, the very reason we name ourselves anew is to show our freedom from these petty concerns."

"Petty, indeed!" This talk made Zaryas vaguely uncomfortable. "What of the dam? He told me he doesn't gamble," she remembered. "So it must be a sure thing."

"That means nothing," the Magus said. "Xerlanthor doesn't gamble because he dislikes risks. How will he contrive to manage the necessary risks of this proposal? Would you, my lady, wager on a novice Thumbprint player?"

She parried the question with one of her own. "Are you saying it *won't* work?"

"I suppose the concept is sound enough," the Magus admitted. "Xerlanthor is too good a geomant to be mistaken about that. We spent the whole day checking his calculations. It ought to work. But on such a scale—it's never been done before. No one knows what obstacles might arise in construction. Might it not be too risky a venture to stake Mishbil on? I don't know."

"I don't know either," Zaryas said. "But I do know it can't be done without magian support. If the Order disapproves of a dam my decision is made."

"You can't push the responsibility off onto me," the Magus reproved smiling. "Of course we'll help, whatever you decide. It's our duty. But the truth is I do not know what would be best."

The Sun had set long ago. From where they sat a wedge of star-strewn night sky was visible above the tiled roofs. The first cool breeze of the evening brought in the distant smell of mint. "It's late," Zaryas said. "Tomorrow, bring the map-trays and your notes. You shall propound the advantages of a dam, and I shall call on Xor, chief of our local hydromants, to present the case for reworking the canals. To choose wisely I must understand everything."

Chapter 5: 1 to 3 Arhem

In later life Zaryas always recalled that next day with horror. Numbers, calculations, and measurements flowed readily from her two advisers, but she interrupted frequently, asking, "How accurate is that?" "Are you sure that's how it will be?" She was striving to pin down what could not ever be truly determined by anyone: the ultimate results of each alternative. The matter was greatly complicated by her own emotions. She fought to be impartial, to judge coldly and clearly. The speed and originality of a dam appealed to all her impatient, ardent nature, and so had to be compensated for. Yet then she could not be sure whether she had overcompensated.

The midday pause passed unnoticed, and day declined into evening. Her head ached with exhaustion. At last bald Xor, equally tired and unnerved by being forced to debate his superior, exclaimed, "The future, princess, lies in the palm of the Sun our god! You don't want our surmises, you want fortunetelling!"

The truth of this was so unexpected Zaryas had to choke back a sharp reply. To her horror the choke turned into a hiccup and the hiccup into tears. All of a sudden she was crying.

"Look what you've done." The Magus accused Xor rather unfairly.

"I didn't mean it, princess, I apologize!" poor Xor told her, awkwardly patting her hand.

"Oh, go away," Zaryas sobbed. "Both of you." The magi had no choice but to obey. When they had gone Zaryas gave herself up to self-pity. The thing was impossible. She dared not decide and so perhaps decide wrongly. She cried out against the injustice of events. She leaned her forehead on the table, wailing. The maids, familiar with their mistress' tempers, tiptoed in to bring a half-dozen clean handkerchiefs.

In the end the tempest blew itself out. Zaryas wiped her hot face and went to take a bath. Warm water steeped with sweet bath herbs relaxed the knot of tension in her neck and she soaked until the Sun was low in the sky. She felt drained, loosened, but rather melancholy. "I'm sick of canals and dams," she grumbled, wrapping herself in an old favorite robe. "I wonder what my city's been doing."

High in the angle between the house wall and its slanted tile roof was a small flat area intended to be a cistern. The cistern had never been built, since it almost never rains in Mishbil, but Zaryas had had the trap-door unblocked and now used the spot as a balcony. She liked the privacy—since she had to stand on the closed door, no one could enter against her will. From this perch she could see the glimmering Eye Pool directly below and the terrace somewhat to the right. Beyond was the russet plaited-reed roof of the main marketplace. When she mounted the stuffy little staircase that evening and looked out over her domain the market was just getting its second wind. Much profitable business is transacted in the cool of the evening. A pleasant homely din composed of vendors' cries, copper-working hammers, the squeal of pigs, and the rattle of wagon wheels drifted to her ear. This was the best time: like an unscheduled star the first lamp was kindled in a booth or shop. As if that first light made busy merchants notice the nightfall, thousands of other lamps lit almost immediately after. The golden glow of the marketplace always made the sky seem suddenly very dark blue, almost black, though the first star was not yet visible.

Her mercurial spirits were already lifting. Groping for a scrap of roof tile Zaryas leaned far over the parapet and released it. The fragment fell, plump! into the Eye Pool more than two stories below. There was just enough light left in the sky to highlight the circular ripples running out and then back. The broad oval lily pads bobbed up and down and then floated quietly once more. She wondered what the fish who lived in the Pool made of these sudden portents from heaven. Did their finny herognomers philosophize, their fortunetellers predict disasters? Or did they simply dart out of the way and go on about their fishy affairs? She scrabbled her feet, feeling for another tile, but there were none.

"Here, toss this."

With a squeak of surprise she whirled. There on the tile roof sloping down behind her perched Xerlanthor, holding out a scrap of tile. "How did you get here?" she demanded.

"The Magus said you were unhappy," he said, sliding down. "So when I saw you come out I lifted up to give you a present."

"Very kind of you," Zaryas thanked him. There was not really room for two in her little niche, and the present was a large heavy bundle wrapped in cloth. She untied it and shook it open. "How lovely!" she cried. "It's a leopardskin, isn't it? A sand leopard!"

It's one of the ones we met on the way here," he said. "The one I wanted to tame. We thought it would be a pity to waste the hide, and brought it to the city to be tanned."

"It's turned out beautifully," she said. The golden fur had a rich silvery sheen and a pure white fluff beneath the longer guard hairs. It was supple as silk, and the tanner had set agates of the exact proper yellow hue in the eye-sockets. "I shall keep it at the foot of my bed." He smiled at that. She realized her saffron linen robe was frayed at the hem where she had once caught it in a door. Pushing back the damp tangled braids over her shoulders, she said, "Excuse my appearance, I didn't expect a visitor here."

"You must rather excuse me," he said politely. Suddenly, unreasonably, she feared he saw she wore nothing under the robe. The blush that rose in her face seemed to scorch right down to her wrists and bosom. To hide it she leaned again over the parapet.

The marketplace was so bright now it cast a yellow stain on the night sky. The Moon, not quite full, peeped over the rooftops to her left, silvering the tiles and bleaching out the green good-luck designs painted under the eaves. Then with an exclamation of annoyance Zaryas pointed southeast at another house. "Look at those boys! Stealing plums again—" Sticking two fingers into her mouth she leaned even farther out and whistled shrilly. "Stop that, you little thieves!" she shouted. "Or I'll have the guardsmen after you!"

Xerlanthor laughed as the shadowy perpetrators started and dashed away. "That's right, put fear into them."

"No lad ever does it more than once, but new ones try every year," Zaryas told him. "The garden wall should be raised a few courses, but that owner's been too lazy." She slid back and almost trod on his toe. As she twisted for balance he steadied her by the wrist. The sudden touch on her bare skin tingled through her. His other hand tipped her face upward. With a maddening, delicious languor his lips sought her forehead, her closed eyelids, and at last found her mouth.

When the breathless moment ended, they turned by common consent to look out over the city again, side by side. Zaryas' heart thumped in her chest so that she could not speak. She was glad to hear Xerlanthor's quick ragged breathing. He took up the bit of tile he had found and gave it to her, asking, "Do you plan to think about canals this evening?"

She smiled, but was too shy to look directly at him. "No, I've worked all day on them. Would you—" But she did not continue, and instead turned the scrap of white-glazed tile over in her palm.

When he saw she would not speak, Xerlanthor slid one arm round her shoulders. "Would you care for company then?"

She ought, Zaryas knew, to think calmly and seriously—of her duties, of his magian responsibilities, of reasons, motives. But her own body betrayed her. A hot intoxicating pulse thrummed in her veins. The warmth of the solid arm around her, of the firm male flank against her own, vied with the cool of the stone parapet against her stomach. Of its own accord her head snuggled into the angle between his ear and shoulder.

The moment of decision slipped by almost unnoticed, but sensing her assent Xerlanthor stroked the fine short hair back from her brow and kissed it. "Come, let's go down." He glanced round. "How *do* we get down?"

"It's a trap-door," Zaryas laughed, a little breathlessly. He bent and raised it. The door was hinged to lean against one wall, and the opening left only a narrow ledge all around. He bundled the leopardskin under one arm, descended a few steps, and held out a hand for her. "Oh, wait!" Zaryas exclaimed. She turned back and leaned far over the parapet again. The fragment of tile he had given her fell from her hand to strike the Pool with a faint splash and gurgle. But it had grown too dark to see its fall, and the ripples marched across the water invisible to straining eyes.

For the past four years Zaryas had slept alone. He was the first man she had brought to the white-plastered bedchamber, set five steps below ground-level to ensure coolness. Very gently Xerlanthor loosened her braids and slid off her robe, and because she saw he enjoyed this she allowed him to undress her like a doll. But when she was naked she leaped on him and half-dragged him to the bed on its low stone platform. "There's no hurry," he gasped laughing as he tumbled backwards onto the cushions.

"Oh, there is," Zaryas told him, tugging at his clothing. Even at that moment an uninvolved side of her noted that she was now one of the very few women who could boast of having stripped a magus. "Every moment is precious. The sky might crack, the river might flood, and forestall us." He made no further argument, but rather responded to her urgency by guiding her hands to the waist-string. She could not be bothered with the rest of the fastenings. It was sufficient, more than sufficient, to possess him partially dressed. Release flowed into sleep so quickly she could barely draw the covers up.

She woke with a start, overheated by the smooth alien flesh against her own. The high-set square windows were faintly outlined with the clear blue light that precedes true sunrise. With a twinge of guilt she pushed the covers back and eased a creased red sleeve from under her hip. In his sleep Xerlanthor fumbled for her warmth, but when she slid next to him became quiet again. His red cap lay forsaken beside the bed. The disheveled robe and gaping trousers gave him a weird, unnaturally debauched appearance. All Zaryas' misgivings rose up at the sight, and she tucked the light quilt over them both again to hide it.

She did not fear censure. Love in Averidan is held rather lightly; the national passions revolve around food. What she dreaded was the fuss—the tidbits of gossip coaxed or bribed out of her servants, the sly glances when she appeared in public, the oblique, envious questions. Rumor and gossip would froth to a hysteria of interest when it came out that she had a lover, redouble when it was learned he was a magus. And what of the canals, the dam? With a sinking heart she foresaw the lurid representation that would seize popular imagination—that Xerlanthor had bought approval of the dam in her bed.

Then a horrid new idea occurred to her. Suppose he had really done so? Had made love to her with the express intention of influencing her judgment? She could not believe it, and yet it seemed all too possible. The affair had been too convenient, too opportune. He had used her for his own ambitious ends. Instinctively now she divined why he had kept his plans quiet until the most dramatic moment—so that Xerlanthor alone should get credit for Xerlanthor's ideas.

All of a sudden his nearness seemed unendurable, the faint odor of sweat and the sticky residue of passion on the sheet. She threw back the covers and flung herself out of bed. A bath, she decided, was necessary to clarify the mind. But when she turned to cover him again, she saw the black-enameled clasp that had pinned his sash torn loose—or had she herself ripped it free? It pressed against his chest, imprinting a red mark on the firm, slightly plump flesh. She bent to undo the pin, steadying her shaking hands by an effort of will so as not to wake him. But suddenly strong clever fingers closed over her own.

"How dear of you," he said softly. "Most uncomfortable, sleeping in clothes. Help me take them off." He tugged on her captive hands till she fell to the bed again.

When he shrugged free of his red robe his skin clung moistly to her breast. She turned her face away from his seeking mouth to demand, "Why are you doing this?"

"Guess," he murmured. He kicked off the rest of his clothes and she gasped as he weighted her body with his own.

"No!" She squirmed from under and retreated to the far side of the bed, trembling. But he kept hold of her hand, distracting her by running his thumb up and down the palm and wrist.

"What is it?"

She regained her courage. "Are you hoping to take advantage of this?"

For a moment his round face was slack with

incomprehension. Then he dropped her hand as if it burnt him. "Is that the rumor?" he demanded harshly.

"It's what everyone will say," she evaded.

"What do *you* say?" She could not meet his eyes, the look of hurt and outrage in them. In the heat of his anger she could not quite believe it after all. However convenient their union had been, his first thought had not been of personal advantage.

In silent fury he began gathering up his discarded garments. "I love you." He seemed to throw the words at her. "But if that's what you believe there's nothing I can say."

But now that he was naked he looked a man only, not a magus. Zaryas had long been able to manage men. She bristled among the rumpled covers like a rudely awakened cat. "We have to face it," she snapped. "Rumor is as real an aspect of government as canals—or dams. More so, in Averidan."

"I don't need to bribe anyone with sex to win approval for the best idea," he retorted. "Tell the truth—in your own best judgment, doesn't my plan outpace all the others?"

"Of course it does," she said. "But that's not the point. Whatever is done, you'll go back to the capital afterward. But I'll run Mishbil all my life. If my people don't trust my integrity—"

She stopped as he began to laugh. "My dear lady," he gasped. "All you needed was to sleep on the decision." He tossed the red bundle into a far corner and lay luxuriously supine on the bed again. "Come and make love," he said and, when she hesitated, added, "You've decided, haven't you? The rest is irrelevant."

His face looked up at her, weirdly exciting upside down on the pillow at her clenched knees. She wavered, knowing that she really had not decided, not in the wise and disinterested way she had wished to. His clever hands explored up her thighs, to probe imploringly at the deep tender crease joining leg and torso. Suddenly the heat of desire made her dizzy and blind. With a moan of either relief or resignation she relaxed and let her knees part.

The Council, gathered next day for Zaryas' decision, seethed with cheerful gossip. In the happily divisive fashion of Viridese almost half of those waiting in the viceroy's hall already approved of their ruler's rumored lover. "If he sacrifices faithfully to Ennelth, he might keep her too busy to pare the accounts so close," the Master Metalworker confided to a petty shipowner. "Maybe they'll even wed." Another party strongly disagreed, principally because they had brothers, sons, uncles, cousins or friends who had hoped to occupy the favored role one day. "Are there not husbands aplenty locally?" a mother of three sons demanded. "One would think Mishbil a city of women and old men." And a small but vocal minority repeated to one and all the old superstition that meddling with magi is unlucky. "Especially in matters of sex," the youngest lord said, serene in his many virile conquests. "There must be a reason they abstain. It has to do with their powers."

Speculation about the viceroy's private life led to guesses about her decision. Bets were already laid, and the more inveterate were busily circulating and increasing their stakes.

When the Magus entered, discussion darted, after an awkward moment of silence, to the crops or the possibility of rain. Here was one who probably knew the decision. And it might after all also be that the Master Magus knew nothing yet of his assistant's affair. To learn of it through public talk might embarrass the Magus. Worse yet, he might utterly scotch the rumor with some evidence, say, of Xerlanthor spending yesterday upcountry surveying dam sites. Inquisitive ears noted the Magus' every word and sharp glances positively skinned each red-clad arrival, in case he should be Xerlanthor. There was always the delicious hope that the effects of a day and two nights of amorous endeavor would be plainly visible on the young magus' face. "He can't be in very much practice," the inveterate young lord whispered, and was hushed by his elders.

Zaryas had foreseen the avidity of her Council's interest and planned accordingly. She entered at the far end of the hall with a rustle of silk sleeves, smiling and greeting those nearby as usual. At that exact moment, while every eye was turned away, Xerlanthor slipped in the main door and sat down among his colleagues.

"I have studied the matter earnestly," Zaryas began, "and find only one safe solution for

Mishbil." The Council leaned forward. The gamblers among them held their collective breath. "Our chief care must first be to ensure our city's water. Therefore, surveying a site for a dam shall begin immediately." She held up one hand for silence as a murmur of comment began. "But while the dam is constructed the canals shall be re-worked also."

A babble of questions and exclamations arose. Only Xantallon seated beside his friend was close enough to see the surprise on Xerlanthor's face. The Master Magus rose and asked, "How shall you afford both options when canals alone are so costly?"

"We'll stop re-digging the canals the moment the dam is proved to be effective," Zaryas said, and added, "As you can see, we're hedging our bets."

This sentiment was readily embraced by gamblers and non-gamblers alike. All-or-nothing bets were fun, but not with the Dragon of Mishbil. It was the sort of typically split-minded decision, embracing two opposing alternatives, that all Shan love. "How dreadfully clever," the matriarch said. "And *safe*." The Master Metalworker rapturously added together the tool estimates for both projects and decided to treat himself to a new wing on his workshop. The Magus rubbed his aching head, foreseeing a more-than-doubled burden of magic work.

But when Xerlanthor rose everyone fell silent, to hear better. "Princess," he said, "the only flaw with this admirable plan is that resources for canal-remodeling must be diverted from the dam. The work is already expensive and risky. Should the city handicap it further?"

"Curse the man," Zaryas muttered under her breath, and then smiled very sweetly on him. "As I said, Mishbil's welfare is my first concern. It is worth any extra labor and cost, and I am sure the Council agrees with me. You have my decision," she said to them. "What do you say?"

The Council gave its official approval and hastily adjourned, brimming with the thrilling news. "A snub, a distinct snub!" the youngest lord whispered in delight. "So soon for their first spat!"

"And not the last, either," the Master Metalworker predicted. "Perhaps I should sacrifice to Ennelith myself, on the young magus' behalf. He'll need all the luck he can muster. Did he look worn, or didn't he?"

Chapter 6: The rest of Summer

Xerlanthor had so firmly linked himself to the dam in everyone's mind that the Master Magus had to give over supervision of it to him. Symmetry then demanded that Xantallon be given authority over the canal renovation project. "They've been friends, not rivals," the Magus reassured himself. "And I will keep an eye on everything."

The canalworks were easy to begin. They were merely a grander and more ambitious version of what every farmer continually did under magian guidance—maintain his waterways. The most convenient canal branch to begin on, in a neighborhood called Five Larches, did not even need to be blocked off from the Bilcad's flow. It had been left high and dry last year. Digging began immediately, the labor proportionately supplied by the owners of the lands benefiting from each canal section. The curved canal bottoms were to be carved into even, trapezoidal cross-sections. Stone slabs to line the newly deepened sections were supplied by the city. After the usual bitter argu-

ment between magi, stone-cutters, and metalworkers, compromise was reluctantly achieved.
Identical table-sized granite slabs were faceted
precisely as gemstones and began to flow in a
slow oxcart procession from the Stonecutters'
Street.

With their glass wands and enchanted basins
of river-water, the hydromants supervised the
work, ensuring the correct slope and level of the
canal. The work was completely familiar to Zaryas
when she came to see it. "In a properly designed
canal," Xantallon told her, "the water should
flow as sweetly as the blood runs in your veins."

The grilling Sun heated the dry canal-trench
until Zaryas felt her head would burst. The odor
of sweat and dried sludge was sour in her nose.
She paced back and forth, taking in the lay of the
land. Five Larches centered around a tavern of
the same name noted for its sugary pastries. The
larches shaded a dining terrace near the canal,
and also featured prominently on the tavern-sign.
The dozen cottages of the village were clustered
nearby.

Zaryas stepped carefully over the first new-
laid stones, and then squatted to speak to the
workman in the next section. He was busy smoothing the earth for the next block. "How long does
each stone take?" she wanted to know. "You're
one of the tenants hereabouts, aren't you?"

The man straightened and spat out grit before
replying. "Yes, I am, princess. It takes several
days to scrape the channel down to the right

depth and shape. But I know the way of it now. Thank Viris my stint is nearly up."

"And who shall your replacement be?"

"My neighbor Chorzin," the man said. His grin showed cheerfully gap-toothed. "I don't envy our red-hat friends. Chorzin's been simple since birth."

"It doesn't seem very efficient," Zaryas agreed. "Since you are likely to be a better worker than Chorzin, would you consider doing his stint as well as your own? For appropriate compensation, of course."

"No, never!" The man shook his rough-cropped head. "It's not the custom at all. And anyway, my cousin's daughter's wedding is next week—"

"All right, never mind," Zaryas interrupted, knowing that the fount of glib excuses could flow forever. "Keep up the standard of your digging. And," she turned back to add with a fine malice, "give the bride my good wishes."

"It's a hopeless effort," Xantallon remarked. "I must say any innovation would make me uneasy. With corvee labor you know exactly where you are."

"Perhaps on an entirely new undertaking we could initiate a different custom," Zaryas said.

"Well," Xantallon said kindly, "you'll have your chance."

Indeed she did. Xerlanthor had firm notions about the custom of corvee. "How can a work be properly done by the unwilling? Of course they'll scamp the labor, get away with as little as they can."

Zaryas was illogically indignant. "Nonsense!" she said. "My subjects work hard and well! They know the future of their farming rests on their labor. And don't parents compel their children to do useful work?"

But her lover would have none of it. "Besides, we magi spend all our time teaching yokels. We'll pay them a token wage. Your people shall willingly labor for the honor and welfare of Mishbil. You'll see."

Not liking this radical proposal, Zaryas had him broach the plan to the Council first. To her secret delight they unanimously disapproved. "We can't afford to pay anybody as it is," a spokesman said. "And what about all those farmers whose canals will never get around to being dug? There aren't crops for them to till. Oughtn't they get off their duffs and do a fair turn? We've innovations enough, let's not cast away all the old customs."

"But at least allot me funds to keep good workers on," Xerlanthor pleaded.

This, Zaryas felt was a laudable end, and she persuaded her Council to put aside a small sum for it. "Not anywhere near enough," Xerlanthor complained later. "How do you expect excellence to be achieved in this atmosphere of niggling?"

"You can persuade the good workers to stay on for a pittance," she comforted. She felt she was learning to manage him. Mere argument made Xerlanthor voluble and stubborn, but he was absurdly easy to outmaneuver, as if the flame of his concentration blinded him to all side issues. He was of course unaware of this, lacking the bent toward introspection that leads to self-knowledge. But Zaryas was happy to observe for two. To know things of him that he himself did not know delighted her as much as knowing of the little balcony on the roof. The magi say that knowledge is power. There were many questions about her lover that promised Zaryas more knowledge, more power. She wanted to know the other Xerlanthor (for there are two minds in every skull, two hearts in every chest)—not the bright warmhearted one that shared her bed, but the hidden one, the one who burned with ambition. How had such an inappropriately driven man become a magus, of all things?

Indirectly she learned the answer to the question one scorching afternoon. They had made love, and almost suffocated in their mingled sweat. When Zaryas had pleaded she was too depleted to stand, Xerlanthor had carried her to the bath, filled it with cool water from the waiting jars, and joined her in it. Sweet herbs steeped in pierced cups all round the tub. But there was plenty of room for two. He had slept pillowed on the mosaic rim, and lulled by the sweet-scented water she had dozed on his shoulder.

Then she sat up and rummaged through the porcelain herb-jars for a blue flask stamped with the seashell-emblem of Ennelith. She had taken a sip of the bittersweet potion when without so much as a warning splash Xerlanthor asked, "Do I get some too?"

"You don't want any, it's not wine," she said,

dropping the glass stopper back into the flask. "This is the infusion the Sodality supplies to the unwed." She put the flash back and settled down into the bath again.

"Don't take any more of it," he said.

She glanced up, surprised at his grave tone. "I haven't the time to bear your child now," she said mildly.

He reached for the flask, turning it to be sure it was the right one. With a sudden furious effort he flung it against the far wall. The glass bottle shattered, splashing an irregular star of greenish fluid on the plaster.

"Xerlanthor!" she gasped, sitting up. But grasping her by the arm he forced her down beside him again.

"Did you know," he asked, "that I can't father a child?"

Astonished, she looked up at his grim face above her. "No, I didn't. Are you sure?"

"I've tried."

"Oh!" So he had achieved only experience, not fatherhood. She tried to think of some positive comment. "Then magery is a good career for you, you needn't worry about offspring." The bitterness of his glance wrung her heart, and resolving to lighten it she added firmly. "You'll certainly leave your imprint on this part of the world."

It was the right thing to say. A real, warm smile melted the brittle tension from his face. Kissing her he said, "I mean to. Not now, of course." Under the attentions of his mouth and hands past and future slipped away. But much later, when Zaryas was combing out her hair, she leaned over the water and saw his strong fingers had left five livid blue marks on her upper arm.

Few in Mishbil had ever seen a dam. No one had ever seen one built. So Xerlanthor managed everything. He chose a site well upstream on the Bilcad between two bluffs, below the lowest canal mouth. It was instantly dubbed "the Neck." "Not the most geomantically suitable site," he judged. "We must make up for the deficient earth currents in the construction." Land on either bank at that point had been commandeered, uprooting three small vegetable farms, a chicken business, and an estate. When Zaryas went out to inspect it nothing was left of these homely concerns. Xerlanthor guided her through a wilderness of raw excavated earth where bare-chested laborers dug ever deeper with bronze picks and others hauled away the earth in baskets. It was too far from town for most of the corvee to walk home every night. So barracks had been erected on either side of the river.

"We'll do it magian fashion," Xerlanthor told her. "Start on either side of the river and work in toward the center of the channel. Like a noose, slowly closing to choke off the water."

"I can't imagine it," Zaryas confessed. It was hard to recall the placid bustle of the farms that used to rule this spot. "The chickens they used to raise over there were delicious, plump and tasty. I hope they'll survive the move. Why do you have to dig everything up? It would have been nice to think of the farms, just as they were, sleeping at the bottom of the lake.''

"The dam must be footed on bedrock," Xerlanthor explained. "It's to be almost thrice as wide as it's high. Without a firm foundation the river currents will undermine it.''

"Geomancy.'' Zaryas dismissed the technical details. She was far more interested in the workmen. "Why does the corvée wear red headbands?''

"That's my idea," Xerlanthor said. "I haven't money to give my men. But I can confer prestige. The really competent get red wristlets, too.''

"It's an idea," she admitted. "What good will that do?''

"Well, I keep an eye on the best, and the most efficient can be installed as foremen.''

"We've never done that," she said. "There aren't any foremen at Five Larches.''

"We use them on dams," Xerlanthor said. "I'm the only one who knows what to do and when to do it. Without reliable deputies I can't possibly manage. Remember, we'll be working on both banks at once. Whereas everyone knows how to dig canals. It's easy.''

When Xerlanthor was called aside to inspect a new draft of workers, Zaryas approached a muscular farm youth who sported both wristlets and headband. It was hard to recognize faces through the sweat and brown dust that digging laid over everything. "What's your name?" she asked.

"Torven-lis Melekirtsan, my lady," he replied, giving the three formal names.

"You aren't a tenant," she said, recognizing

the Tsorish-extraction name. "Have you any call to geomancy, do you think?"

"Oh, no—we're all vinners in our family. But it's an honor to work with my lord Xerlanthor. To help in something so mighty— Long bare arms waved helplessly as Torven tried to find words. "And anyway," he added, patting his belly, "the meals are lovely, nicer than we get at home."

Tradition demanded that every man in the corvee be fed twice a day at public expense. Of course it was proper that Xerlanthor provide his men the best, but not perhaps very prudent. She knew better than to complain about it to Xerlanthor, though, and when he returned she merely asked him, "Is there more you need?"

"Men," Xerlanthor replied. "When we really begin building we'll need hydromants especially, to handle the river. I've talked to the Master Magus about it. Aside from all the other supplies."

She sighed. "Leave it to me."

The costs were frightful. Confident of the market, some stone-quarriers and metal smelters tripled their prices. Zaryas retaliated by declaring all unfairly priced material sole property of the city. Magi, mainly hydromants, were summoned through their mirrors by the Master Magus from the length and breadth of Averidan. Though they were servants of the Shan King and thus demanded no wage, the magi did have to be housed and fed. And the corvee also had to be fed, a growing number of hungry men every day. Grain hoarded against the winter diminished rapidly,

and food began to run short all over Mishbil as
autumn quenched summer's fires.

When she had unsealed the last granary Zaryas
journeyed west to the Neck again. In the weeks
that had passed a vast angled berm of rammed
earth mixed with gravel had begun to nose across
the valley. It was higher than many houses, and
far wider than its height, so that it looked like a
mountain. Or actually, Zaryas reflected, a giant
turd, perhaps the Dragon's dropping. But she
choked back her giggle when she saw Xerlanthor
approach. She never called at the Neck on personal affairs, preferring to entertain her man in
her own comfortable bed rather than the makeshift quarters he used here.

"It'll be a close bet," Zaryas said to him. "When
shall the dam be finished?"

"The water level of the Bilcad will drop as
winter approaches," he said. "When it does, we'll
start—night and day, triple shifts—across the river
bed. The dam will be finished before spring brings
high water again." It was easy to believe his
confident assertion when she looked at the sections already underway. "We're like runners
poised to start a race," Xerlanthor continued.
"Only it's toward ourselves, over there." They
had ascended the berm and picked their way to
the very edge. He pointed across the Bilcad at
the other half of the dam.

Zaryas looked down. The river was stained
brown with dirt from the digging, and seemed
impossibly swift and wide. "You'll meet in the

middle? How will you hold your breath while you dig down there?"

He laughed at her. "Why do you think I've been scraping hydromants from under every rock in Averidan? They'll magically turn the water from whatever section we work on."

She glanced round, noticing the many wielders of glass wands already on both shores busily charting currents or measuring depths. "And there are as many at Five Larches? I didn't know there were so many water-wizards in the country."

"There aren't," he admitted. "So many at Five Larches, I mean. I secured to myself the lion's share. Since his project is less important good old Xerlanthor doesn't need so many magi. There isn't enough of anything to go around."

"As long as you've worked it out with him," Zaryas said. Her mind was running ahead to her errand. "We're running out of barley. If only we had been able to raise a crop this year. Or if only the previous years' crops hadn't been so thin and light."

He must have sensed her loss of confidence, for he said, "Not your fault. It was because the water was diminishing already. Next year you'll have a crop."

"I can send to His Shan Majesty for more grain to see us through till then," she said with a sigh. "But the stakes are getting very high. You understand, we'll be asking other farmers in Averidan essentially to back our gamble."

"I know it," he said. "The only wager I've ever made, too. Shall we raise the stakes higher yet?"

"I don't understand you," she said shortly. The laughter danced in his dark eyes. He did not seem to have grasped the seriousness of the situation.

"If this works, if I save your city—marry me."

Suddenly her depression lifted. The merriment in his smile matched her own now. "You just want to enjoy your greatest work," she teased. "Or no, the workmen have petitioned you to stay. Which is it?"

"Both, partially," he said. He glanced proudly round the work site, before leaning closer. "But chiefly because you are a woman I could love every night of my life."

The sudden murmured avowal was fiercely arousing. The smell of his sweat was rank yet appetizing. "Aren't you tired of living out here?" she whispered. "Come back to the city with me tonight." Very lightly under the shield of her raised wide sleeve he touched her breast, feeling the taut nipple. The dust soiled her thin robe but only the many watching eyes held her from embracing him.

"We are so alike." He breathed in her ear and seeing he shared her excitement, she cast her eyes down. "So, will you?"

"On one condition." He froze, the round muscles of his jaw leaping with sudden tension. His mood of confidence was shattered so quickly she hastened to add, "When we're married don't seduce me at construction sites anymore."

He laughed at that, so joyously that the men

hauling baskets of earth looked back at them. "It's a bargain," he said.

Zaryas discovered Xantallon had other views about hydromants entirely. As if to demonstrate his less-favored status he presented himself at the Justice Chamber where Zaryas settled disputes twice a week. She looked up from fining two handkerchief-snatchers and saw the tall red-clad figure seated at the farthest end of the petitioners' bench. Though she knew it would cause comment she had the chamberlain call him to the head of the line,

"Well, Xantallon," she greeted him cheerfully. "What complaint do you bring, did a wine-shop bilk you?"

"Not precisely," he said. The warmth of so many bodies kept the Chamber stuffy despite its size, and now Xantallon wiped his forehead and sagging black mustache with a dingy square of silk. "I need your judgment, there's a difficulty with the corvee. It seems any farmer who wishes may work on the dam instead of the canals."

"That's right," Zaryas said cautiously. "It's a new idea, Xerlanthor's. He wants the corvee at the dam to *want* to work on it. There's been no difficulty with it so far."

"But when I came to one farm to levy workers for the canal the owner told me his stint was already done—that his men were working for Xerlanthor." Xantallon seemed quite shocked.

"Surely there are enough workers for you both," Zaryas said.

"Well, it's only fair that the canals be dug by those who use it," Xantallon pointed out. "That's the proper way. On the other hand, no one should have to work two turns. Yet what would become of the Five Larches branch if everyone farming near it went to work at the Neck?"

"I can see your point," she said soothingly. "It's difficult to have two corvee systems at once. Suppose I rule that no one served by the Five Larches canal may work on the dam anymore. Perhaps the situation won't arise again." She spoke very firmly, and gestured to the chamberlain for the next case, so that Xantallon had no choice but to accept her decision.

Chapter 7: Autumn

Between the demands of two magian works Mishbil had to tighten its collective belt. The realization that in more fortunate parts of the realm the harvest season was at its peak weighed unspoken on every heart. It was hard to look forward to spring so far away, when the dam should be finished. Despite rigid grain doles a black market in barley flour sprang up. Farmers averted their eyes from the barren fields. In town handwatered vegetable gardens became the mode. Stylish ladies who had deemed parsnips a peasants' vegetable learned to discourse about mulch and the virtues of cow manure. The farm lads who gathered wild onions and flowering spinach did a roaring trade until even the farthest, most arid valleys had been stripped of edible growth.

Zaryas labored to keep every belly filled, fining hoarders and actually ordering the lapidation of a speculator. The number of stones piled over the criminal's rocky bed testified to public anxiety. No one truly hungered—there were still fish

in the sea and mussels in the river for the taking—
but the eerie specter of future famine transformed
food from a love to an uneasy obsession. Even
Zaryas found herself savoring each shellfish, picking every fishbone clean, as if she could squirrel-
like save up nourishment in herself. In this
atmosphere of subdued panic the rumors that
burgeoned were perhaps inevitable.

People knew and loved—and feared, a little—
their princess. Did she not nurture them in famine, nag them to labor at what was good for
them? The deeply conservative Shan, happy under their preternaturally just King, were strang-
ers to revolution. But that very dislike of change
was now perpetually annoyed, and the annoyance perforce focused round Xerlanthor—the author of strange innovations, a prominent mover
in all this undignified upset, so unlike a magus.
Xantallon's work at Five Larches was pointed
out as the proper sort of thing for magi to do. As
Zaryas had foreseen, it was impossible to eradi-
cate the popular suspicion that Xerlanthor was
exploiting her. Yet the typical Viridese two-
mindedness allowed criticism to envelop Xerlanthor but leave Zaryas untouched. She was not
sure she approved of this unfairness, though it
did make managing the city much easier.

Things came to a head the day a fleet of barges
brought in a shipment of fine granite from the
mountain mines. Zaryas went down with her
treasurer to pay the quarriers. As the sedan chairs
neared the river-quay she saw a lean red-clad
figure teetering from barge to barge—Xantallon,

selecting canal slabs. He waved at her as the
bearers set her down.

The quarrier in charge bowed deep before
Zaryas, and made stiff polite conversation as
she looked over the tally scrolls. "It's snowing
already in the mountains, my lady," he told
her.

"Hard to believe," she replied absently. In
Mishbil the heat had just begun to temper.

"Oh, yes—fact! It'll be a cold and snowy season if this first taste is any guide."

"It all looks in order," Zaryas said, tying the
scroll back up. "Let's see the shipment." She
knew little of judging granite quality but a careful inspection was her duty.

"Princess!" Torven, Xerlanthor's foreman,
hailed her from the roadway above. She waited
for the young man as he raced down the ramp to
the quay.

"What energy you have," she said praising
him.

"Xerlanthor sent me to look at the stone," he
panted.

The quarrier frowned so that the loose skin
pursed into flabby parentheses around his mouth.
"The other magus is culling granite for the canals," he told Torven. "You must wait your turn."

"Oh, but my lord Xerlanthor gets priority,"
Torven announced with innocent self-importance.

The barge-men and quayside loiterers who
heard this hooted. "You should have had My
Lord come down himself," one idler mocked. "A
quarrel between magi would have been exciting."

But one in a red headband retorted, "Empty heads ring as loud as empty bellies."

"Indeed so!" another snapped back. "Look at the shoulders on your friend! He's well fed—and back him against the thin magus up there."

Torven scowled indiscriminately around. The embarrassed quarrier tried to shepherd Zaryas toward the first barge, saying, "Pay no attention to these low-lifes, my lady, it just encourages them to make trouble."

"Wait!" she protested. "What did they mean, well fed?"

The little crowd, which had shown signs of division, united now in indignation. "That sleek reptile is deceiving her!" "You can tell he's more concerned about that dam."

Zaryas pointed at the nearest barge-man. "You, there," she ordered, "tell me the rumor."

The man glanced uneasily at her and then avoided her eye. "The story's up and down the river," he said, "that the magi get more than their rightful share."

"Of food?"

The man nodded. "Especially *those*, the ones with red bands who work with the magus Xerlanthor."

Torven bristled in defense of his master. "That's an accursed lie, you jealous, narrow-minded lout!" he exclaimed and, grabbing the barge-man by the scruff, threw him off the quay into the river. The water was only chin deep, and floundering up to the mud-bank the barge-man scooped up a handful of runny black ooze.

With deadly accuracy the mud hit Torven square in the face.

Zaryas could not help laughing at the sight of the brawny foreman wiping black slime out of his eyes. To her dismay the spectators took this for approval, and leaped down the embankment for more ammunition. Instantly the air was full of hurtling river mud. Torven staggered back under the barrage, and Zaryas and the quarrier took shelter behind the barge house.

"They'll kill him!" she cried.

"A little mud never hurt anybody," the quarrier said unsympathetically.

Blinded, Torven swung a fist at one of his assailants, tripped on a bale, and fell off the quay into the river. His whooping foes ducked him and rolled him over and over on the sticky mudflat. "Stop that, he'll drown!" Zaryas shouted, but her voice was lost in the jeering laughter and splashing.

On a farther barge she saw Xantallon's astonished face peering out over a stack of slabs. She whistled to catch his attention. "Xantallon, do something," she cried, and stamped in fury when he ducked nervously out of sight again. She turned again to the quarrier. "We can't let them lynch him," he's a Melekirtsan."

The quarrier softened at this appeal to snobbery. "All right, then," he said. An unshipped steering-oar made a good flail. While the quarrier whacked heads and backs Zaryas leaped overside to find Torven and drag him to safety.

Immediately she realized her mistake. The mud

of the river bed had been churned up until the
water was thicker than soup. She could feel no
solid bottom under her feet, but only an endless
warm depth of mud that clung grimly to everything. Her right sandal was sucked down into
the depths, and she paddled hard to keep her
head above the ooze. The grime disguised everybody. How could she even recognize Torven?
She floundered to a shallower spot and lost her
other shoe.

The mud had run down her forehead, and she
made a futile effort to wipe her face on her
sleeve. She froze. Her hand came away not black
with mud but scarlet. It was blood, red arterial
life-blood. Had she cut herself somehow on a bit
of submerged glass or metal? But when she looked
down she saw she was waist-deep in blood. The
mud-bank looked like a charnel-house, the riot-
ers like corpses.

With a yell of horror someone clawed up the
side of a barge and scurried away. Zaryas almost
retched at the sight of the clotted sticky hand-
prints on the planking. Shuddering, she tried to
follow but could get no purchase on the smooth
wood. Someone gave her a boost, and when she
was up she gave her helper a hand. Though it
was plainly a trick of some sort—for where was
the reek of gore, the many corpses who must
have bled to death? —the eye and belly insisted
on taking the warm sticky stuff as blood. Chilled
and sobered, the angry crowd melted away.

"Are you hurt, my lady?" A frightfully maimed
figure loomed up beside her. It wiped handfuls

of clotted gore from its head and revealed itself as Torven.

"Viris save us all," Zaryas gasped. He had a black eye but seemed unwounded.

"Whatever happened?" he demanded.

"It's magery," she decided. Breathing deeply to calm her nausea she led the way across the barges. There, seated comfortably on a slab was Xantallon. His thick glass wand was poised in his hand, but when he saw Zaryas he lowered it. "What did you do?" she asked him.

"A hydromant's parlor trick: transmogrification," he said shyly. "I hope it was the kind of help you needed."

She looked down at herself. Now that the glass wand had fallen blood clots had turned to lumpy black mud again. She was mired from chin to heels. "You mean it was just illusion?"

"Nothing more than appearance," he admitted.

She noticed him tugging at the limp black mustache to hide his smile. All of a sudden their horror and surprise seemed very funny. "So it was mud all the time," she said with a giggle. "What dolts we must have looked!"

"We still do," Torven said. He was plastered thick with black mud, and looked like a black beeswax statue left on a hot stove. "But I intend to look this shipment over anyway." He glared at Xantallon as if expecting belligerence.

The magus met his stare. "It's not mannerly, foreman, to quarrel with your rescuer," Xantallon said in deceptively mild tones. "I've seen all I wish of the granite here. I'll discuss its division with Xerlanthor—and the Master Magus."

With that he turned away. But Zaryas ran after him, her wet robe sloughing gobs of mud at every step. "Don't be angry, Xantallon," she begged. "Oh, I can't touch you, I'll come off on your clothes. All this is just love of argument— you know the way we are. It means nothing."

From his greater height Xantallon could look solemnly down his lean nose at her. "Do you think that?" he said quietly. "Our quarrelsome customs can disguise genuine conflict until all possibility of reconciliation is past. Xerlanthor is splitting the city, dividing the Order. Is this what you want?"

"No," she said. She could not account for the chill his quiet words laid on her heart. "You were right. I shall have the Master Magus judge between the two of you."

He bowed to her, as elaborately as if she were not barefoot and filthy—an ironic salute. "That would only be proper," he said, "since your own impartiality is no longer plain."

But somehow the idiotic battle eased public tensions a little. The laugh was more relaxing than wine. And the Master Magus did indeed smooth over the supply dispute, at least on the surface. Zaryas took swift advantage of the lull, fearing it might be only a prelude to the storm. She broached her ideas to Xerlanthor one evening in her office, where they were approving requisitions. Desire was only one reason why he always arrived late in the evenings. The other, Zaryas realized, was that every daylit hour had to be spent at the Neck.

The scrolls went from his stack, under his ink-brush, and then to her stack and her brush, in a weary grind that reminded Zaryas of the baskets hauling earth back and forth. "I must go to the capital this winter," she told him. "It's, what? twenty days to winter solstice? I have formal audience that day with the Shan King. You must come too."

"My dear lady, I can't." Xerlanthor protested without looking up from the scroll he was initialing. "Next week we begin the race across the channel. Midwinter would be the very worst possible time."

"It's necessary," Zaryas said, "if you are to be my consort. His Majesty must approve our union. Ah, and we must announce the betrothal very soon, before discontent rises again. That is," she added, "if you're still of the same mind."

"It's hard to be convincing in this setting," he said dryly, "but I am."

"Good." Her dark eyes were abstracted, seeing only the political niceties. "You start damming the channel next week? Let's get up a little ceremony of some sort, and announce the betrothal then. We'll make it an official occasion—dress up, get the Mistress to make offerings, and so on. To link you officially with me might save a lot of fuss."

"I'll agree to that," Xerlanthor said evenly. "And you know I want to wed you. But I cannot leave the work at midwinter." He rolled up the signed scroll, put it on the stack awaiting Zaryas, and reached for another. "You make too much of this fuss. It's merely Xantallon's petty jealousy. Ignore it and he'll go away."

A dozen arguments bubbled to her lips, but Zaryas said only, "His Shan Majesty would be interested to meet you, I'm sure."

That made him look up. "I've only met King Varim twice," he remembered. "Never to speak to, but always in a large group. Haven't you always wondered about his Crystal Crown?"

"Only you can explain the dam to the King properly," she tempted. "And by then a little voyage would do you good. The Master Magus could manage the construction for the three or four days we'd be gone."

"I suppose I could leave him a schedule of instructions," Xerlanthor mused. Zaryas bent busily over her scrolls to hide her smile.

The Shan adore ceremony. Furthermore, whatever their feelings everyone in Mishbil burned with curiosity about the Dam. The turnout for the sacrifice there delighted Xerlanthor. But with her more experienced eye Zaryas spotted the flowers and copper coins that were furtively thrown into the sullen waters. Ennelith Sea-Mother commands open respect. Zaryas thought she know who was offered these sly bribes. "Oh, well, today should satisfy the Dragon too," she grumbled to herself. "Even though the sacrifices are dedicated to Ennelith."

A gritting wind tugged at her ornate sleeves as Zaryas led the procession up the slope to the top of the mound. Under the long full robe she wore practical work boots lest she slip on the mud. The Sodality of Ennelith was waiting atop the great earthen berm. In their many shades of blue they looked like a rack in a dyer's storeroom. Today for the first time Xerlanthor walked beside her. His strong callused hand was warm under her elbow as he helped her up the slope.

On top the wind was downright cold. She could see the bright-clad crowd thronging below, and a cheerful buzz of comment rose when they saw her. A plank platform covered the construction at the verge so that worthies would not have to scramble for footing on the raw edge of the growing dam.

The sacrifices were chosen to either float or dissolve, lest something should be sacrilegiously recovered when the Bilcad was dammed. Carved wooden plaques of farm scenes, soft plaster images of farm beasts, and a grand gaudily tinted representation of the city of Mishbil done in flour-starch and hard sugar—everything was a hint to the goddess of where attention should be directed.

When all was ready the Mistress of the Sodality stepped forward to address the crowd. "Mishbil is fortunate in her viceroy and princess," the Mistress began. "On this fortunate day she has a further announcement. The lady Zaryas has chosen a spouse. She will wed the magus Xerlanthor next summer."

There was a murmur of surprise. Not even rumor had suggested the princess was so far gone. But Zaryas sensed a kind of relief. It was good to have the relationship publicly acknowledged. The Shan prefer order and performance. And now there was the prospect of a grand wedding to look forward to.

Booming copper bells green with verdigris were then struck to attract the goddess' attention. The clamor was deafening. Since Ennelith is not a goddess of words no prayers were made. The offerings were thrown downstream into the river, and the bells were stilled by many hands so that they could be accepted in the customary silence. The plaques glided down to the brown water and sank briefly before resurfacing and floating away. The plaster figures dropped with scarcely a splash and vanished. But to everyone's embarrassment the confectionary city hit a shallow spot and stuck forlornly half out of the muddy water. Gradually the current dissolved it and the frosting towers and miniature cloth flags sagged out of sight. The crowd fidgeted, chilled and depressed by the unpropitious delay, but short of pelting the reluctant offering with stones there was nothing to be done.

The instant the offering was gone Xerlanthor signaled to the farther bank. In response the waiting hydromants that he had purloined from Xantallon waded knee-deep into the chilly water. Zaryas strained her eyes but saw only the distant flutter of red robes in the current, and the thick glass wands poised in their hands. Then, very slowly, the river current curved, not from the edges into the middle as she had expected, but to one side. The magi on this side retreated as the water thrust up to their chests. "To scour the riverbed clean," Xerlanthor explained. "Why work to dig out the silt when the Dragon will wash it away for us? We'll swing the force of water from one side to the other as we advance."

The sight of the river curving unnaturally up the slope was unnerving. Leaving Xerlanthor to his work, Zaryas descended with the Sodality. The Mistress walked beside her. There is a strength that stems from abstention, like that wielded by the warrior Sisters or the mild magi. But the power of Ennelith is that found in experience, in deep draughts from the well of knowledge. Though the Mistress was a slim slight woman younger than herself Zaryas knew that she was a fit and apt vessel for the divinity. Like the sea her patroness, the Mistress was a safe repository of secrets. Zaryas was startled to hear her own voice quietly asking, "Do you think I'm doing the right thing?"

The Mistress' dark-eyed glance held surprise. "Do you mean the dam, or *him*?"

"I don't know," Zaryas confessed. "Whatever it is, it's too late now."

"Whatever it is, we trust your judgment," the Mistress said soothingly, but it was not much comfort to Zaryas.

The remnant of the year was swept away by the torrent of construction. The proper way to build things in Averidan is deliberately, over time, with due pauses for wars, festivals, accumulating more money, or simply thinking it over. Instinctively Xantallon so managed the canal-works. But the dam completely eclipsed that gentle labor. Zaryas found it hard to grasp that she had somehow begot this grueling, foreign style of labor. Nearly every able-bodied laboror in Mishbil was pressed into the corvee. She watched them set out shift by shift to haul earth and gravel and stone, and creep back perhaps a week later— having slept out on the site—drained, consumed. She had felt the same impotence when the *Silver Gull* was lost. Mishbil writhed in the grip of swift mighty forces she could not see or master.

As she tested the temper of her city Zaryas realized she had yoked her fortunes to Xerlanthor in more ways than one. If the dam paid off all would be forgiven. The life-blood of Mishbil was worth any cost, any effort, she had said, and truly. She, and Xerlanthor, would be hailed as saviors. But if by some unimaginable misfortune the gamble was lost Zaryas would be liable for all—from every blistered hand and aching back to the entire fearful mass of stone and earth that choked the Dragon. Win or lose, she had staked everything now on Xerlanthor.

With all these reflections rasping at her nerves it was difficult to leave him to his work. The magi were hardly seen at all, and Xerlanthor himself spent weeks at a time on site. She glimpsed him rarely, on his hasty infrequent trips into town, but resisted the temptation to go out to the Neck.

Once when she went to bed she found him tumbled on a couch beside the bath. Exhaustion had overtaken him before he could wash. As she watched him sleep two impulses warred within her. He was hers; she ought to take care of him, force him to rest. Yet since so much depended on his labor, ought she to hold him back? In the end she let him sleep. Winter solstice was very soon, surely he could rest then.

Chapter 8: Mid Winter Day

This time Zaryas chose a good ship for the voyage north, captained by a well-seasoned man. Xerlanthor exerted himself at the Neck up to the very hour of departure. Zaryas sent a sedan chair to fetch him lest the sailing tide ebb. But when the last good-bye had been waved to the harbor folk, and when sprawling Mishbil had slipped away astern he tucked one arm around her waist and sighed, "How can it have been so long?"

The salt sea-air did not quite mask the faint delicious smell of his flesh and hair. "I have my own cabin this trip," she said in his ear.

Once such happiness would have made her uneasy. Nothing has been unalloyed since the beginning when the Sun joined his incandescent life with cool Ennelith's nature. Thus all that exists is two-souled, at war with itself. But on that voyage Zaryas delighted in the joy that poured over them, undilute, unmixed. It seemed hardly possible to muffle the fire of their ecstasy in the narrow cabin's narrower bed. Yet the exaltation was no less palpable in sitting handfast on the steering-deck to watch the Sun set, and wait for the first sight of the City. "Shall we always be so happy?" she asked him, more to hear his voice than to get an answer.

"It's of no importance," he replied. "Now, this moment, is all you can encompass. You taught me that. Embrace it, drink it dry, while it's yours."

"Oh, I shall." She hugged him, compressing the firm-padded ribs under his red linen robe until he wriggled in protest. "But I will remember today forever."

"And tonight." He nodded at their destination, the Palace and Temple a shining-bright crown over the purple-dark Lower City. "I hope His Shan Majesty allotted us a large bed."

"He will," Zaryas said with confidence, and when they docked and presented themselves at the Palace they found it was so. "I'm a prophet-ess," Zaryas gloated as they retired.

It was strange yet delightful to sleep so high, and to wake with the Sun picking out flecks of white fire on the azure sea so far below. "Let us build our marriage chamber where your little balcony is now," Xerlanthor proposed, "so that we can see all Mishbil, and the sky."

"And bake like raisins in the summertime," she retorted. "You are the most impractical man."

For the audience Zaryas dressed with care, brushing and braiding her black hair until it was arranged smooth and intricate as carved granite. Her maids had shaken out and smoothed the white-and-green formal robe. After donning it she uncovered the great square mirror for a quick glimpse of herself. Her narrow sharp face seemed newly softened with happiness, oddly at variance with the dignified trappings of power. "Have I changed?" she asked aloud. "I don't want to change."

"The gray threads lend a distinguished air," her maid said helpfully. "But if my lady wishes I know of a preparation whereby blackness may be restored. . . ."

"No, no." Zaryas laughed and gave her place to Xerlanthor. His red linen reflected back plain and humble beside her own splendor. Only the Master Magus wears formal silks. But under the red cap and straight dark hair his gaze met her own with the pride of an equal. She hugged his arm and exclaimed, "What a nice couple we make!"

"I hope His Shan Majesty thinks so," he replied.

They were conducted through the ancient maze of white marble halls to a high roomy chamber, where wide triple-arched windows opened out over the cliff. Below, hundreds of winter-brown fields were knitted together with silvery canals, as far as they could see. The gentle Mhesan, a mighty yet mannerly river, wound away seawards to the left. Here most of all Zaryas felt the weight of the ages, the thousands of years and millions of lives that were Averidan. Surely the Shan were wedded to their land, the one as unchanging as the other. Her forebears had lived the same peaceable, busy lives her children would. The thought was indescribably comforting, as secure and supporting as the rock under her feet. And then she remembered she would have no children, if she wedded Xerlanthor. "I shall make a wish about it," she promised herself, "while I'm here."

Music from the brazen gongs announced the Shan King's arrival. Zaryas had been surprised last summer at his age. The change now was even more startling. Shan Varim King had wasted away. His pale thin skin hung slack over the brittle old bones. The King looked sucked dry, juiceless enough to crack at a hasty step. They rose, and stood until he was helped to his seat.

When she came forward to take the King's outstretched hand Zaryas glanced timidly up at his face. She feared to see the wreckage of mind as well as body, a senile mockery of her old friend. But the dark eyes were bright and knowing as ever.

"Tell me, O my viceroy, of my city Mishbil," the Shan King formally requested. So Zaryas did. She spoke of canals and grain shortages, crime and shipping, barges and fishermen—all the doings of Mishbil for the past year. She submitted tax receipts, financial records, and import manifests, summarizing a year's worth of life in the realm's third-largest city.

Every year Zaryas did this she could not escape the feeling that the Shan King was listening not to her words but to something else she communicated. The gesture of her hands, the smell of her skin, perhaps the tilt of her eyebrows or the way she hunched her shoulders forward—he extracted information she did not know she had, in a way she could not fathom.

When she was done it was nearly noon. In a side chamber a repast was spread. The chamberlain approached to help the old King down from his chair, but Varim waved him back. "No," he commanded. "Lend me the strength of your arm, young magus."

Xerlanthor came forward for the first time and bowed before stepping onto the dias. With a vague unease Zaryas watched the King lean forward to look into Xerlanthor's eyes. The Son of the Sun does not see as others do. But His Majesty remarked only, "So you wish to wed Zaryas of Mishbil, what good taste you have."

During the meal—a vegetable stew flavored with saffron, barley porridge, redfish baked in the northern style, and fruits in cream—they talked of food, the proper way to hang venison and whether cactus-fruit can be pickled into edibility. Only afterwards did the Shan King continue, "It is not unusual for magi to marry."

Zaryas began to speak but held her tongue when Xerlanthor replied, "I am no usual magus. It will be to the princess's advantage to marry me."

Varim glanced at Zaryas before asking, "How so?"

"When the dam reverses Mishbil's agricultural decline I shall get the credit for it," Xerlanthor said. "By wedding me the princess shall share in that acclaim. It is never a disadvantage to associate with a hero."

Zaryas stared. That aspect had never occurred to her before. But the King was saying, "This presumes your very radical plans bear fruit. You must expound them to me." And they adjourned again to the audience chamber.

Zaryas did not attend to Xerlanthor's lecture and the water demonstration with the map-trays. She had other things to consider. Who had been using whom? Had she also a dark, selfish side to her motives? They had both derived such delight from their love that it was hard to recall it was not the whole world. The mutual advantages and disadvantages of the relationship were unseen, like the roots of trees, but necessary to support the luxuriant growth above. She had ignored them, but the Shan King would not. She came to herself in time to hear His Majesty address her.

"My dear Zaryas," he said, "I think you have made a good choice here in Xerlanthor, magus or no. However, I cannot sanction the union until later next year—you understand."

She nodded. "If the project doesn't work, for whatever reason, Xerlanthor would no longer be an asset to me or to you."

"How clear-sighted of you," the King approved, while Xerlanthor cast a pained glance at her. "What other business do you plan to transact here? A wish-sacrifice? Good—let us go through the gardens to the Temple. No doubt you, Xerlanthor, have errands at the Order's headquarters on behalf of your Master?"

Thus dismissed Xerlanthor bowed and withdrew. Zaryas gave the old King her arm and carefully helped him down. The chamberlain hurried to open the tall glassed doors to the terrace, and they walked very slowly across the lawn and down the narrow garden paths. The plantings were asleep for the brief Viridese winter, tidily wrapped in burlap or mulched under dry leaves. A cool Sun flitted in and out of wind-driven cloud, but here on the ground the air was still and frosty. Zaryas curbed her swift pace to match the King's halting step. "Do you feel the cold?" she asked.

"No, no," the King said peevishly. "Zaryas, my dear, how well do you know your Xerlanthor?"

She smiled at him. "Very well indeed," she said.

"Everyone has two sides to his heart," the King said. "I know that is true. Do you?"

"Of course," she said in surprise. "Everyone knows that."

He patted her hand with his own, dry and frail as the dry leaves. "Then do not be astonished when you find that unknown in your intended," he advised.

"I think I have already," she said.

"You have not," said the King. Zaryas did not ask how he had come by that conclusion. "Couples may call themselves fortunate if one side of one speaks to one side of the other. Don't invest your heart too deeply or quickly, my dear. Your pain would be hard to behold." The sentiment from anyone else would have seemed self-centered. But Zaryas recognized it for an oblique expression of regard.

The Kings of the Shan have their own little gate from Palace grounds to the Temple, screened by a few ornamental trees. The white stone of the courtyard beyond retained the warmth of the sunshine. In the strong light the King seemed transparent as wax. "Come in yourself," Zaryas urged, "and make a wish."

"I am Lord of the Shan, Son of the Sun," Varim replied. "What could I lack?"

"Health?" Zaryas suggested boldly.

The King chuckled. "I am an old man," he said. "No wish can lengthen the span of my days. Go in, my dear. I shall wait here." So she sat him down on a bench in the sun-warmed courtyard and went in.

The gold-domed sanctuary was unchanged. Change would have been shocking, for the Temple and its rites are old almost beyond memory, their beginnings veiled in plaiv-borne myth. A white-clad priestess accepted Zaryas' offering—a gilded bracelet carved of sweet-smelling wood. "I wish to conceive by the one I love," she wished, so promptly that the priestess frowned.

"Phrase your wish carefully!" she cautioned. "And be sure to offer to Ennelith also." Zaryas waited patiently for the bracelet to be consumed. This time the flame burned small and blue, nibbling away the gilding until with a puff of yellower fire the wood underneath caught. "The goddess will hear your prayer, if you petition her. I see it clearly," the priestess reported at last.

"All I've asked today has come to me," Zaryas

sighed happily. A gambler's luck seemed to tingle through her fingers. She was confident anything she laid hand to would turn out well. With a light heart she skipped out to the courtyard again. The Shan King smiled at her high spirits. Impulsively she hugged his frail-boned shoulders, as if her own joyous vitality might by an act of will be contagious.

By the time they sailed next day Xerlanthor's mind was again preoccupied with his dam. He spent hours bent over his mirror scrying for a view of the site. "We're still too far away," he fretted. "At least for a middling scryer like myself. This calls for a hydromant."

Zaryas felt no such anxiety. "You can't do anything about what you see anyway, out here on the ocean," she pointed out. But wisely she said no more. It was more important to drink in the brisk cool air and enjoy the holiday. The sky was cold but sunny, its calm wintry blue contrasting with the turbulent gray-blue sea. The unchanging yellow desert on their right seemed to dance—not with heat, but with tiny dust devils. There was hardly a chance of another blinding dust storm, however, for the wind blew off the sea. Though the desert seems sterile it has one harvest. Winter is the season for spices and aromatic gums, and dozens of tents and makeshift shelters along the shore showed the desert's bounty was being gathered. The spice merchants would send donkey caravans through the dunes all this season, only filling their water jars every few days at the infrequent springs. It was also a profitable time for hunters and adventurers, who could hire out as spearmen to guard against sand leopards.

The brief winter day was fading fast when Xerlanthor finally descried the dam. His shout of dismay made sailors startle and Zaryas dash across the slanting deck to his aid. "What is it, what's wrong?" she demanded.

"They've made hardly any progress at all!" he cried. "Look at this!"

Warily she peered into the thick, round mirror. Neither her face nor her surroundings showed, but only a shining mist in which vague colors shifted and blurred. "I'm not a magus," she reminded him. "Why has the work stopped?"

He examined the reflection carefully before announcing, "The magi. Not a hydromant or a geomant do I see."

"How could that be?" Zaryas exclaimed, but Xerlanthor was sure of the answer.

"Xantallon," he said. "Xantallon has stolen all my workers away."

"The Master Magus wouldn't allow that," Zaryas objected.

"He must have." Fury made Xerlanthor's fingers clumsy as he slid the mirror back into its bronze case. "Curse of the goddess be on them both!" His gaze burned into her own, the force of his will almost palpably pressing her. "The Shan King himself approved the dam."

"I'm certain they didn't mean to defy royal authority," Zaryas said. "That's unheard of.

No doubt there's some reasonable explanation—"

"It's treason," Xerlanthor insisted. She had seen such cold rage before only in betrayed wives or cuckolded husbands. A loyalty had been violated. "Isn't it your duty to order lapidation when—"

"Indeed it's my duty," Zaryas interrupted. She had never met this possessive bloodthirsty Xerlanthor before. "You must let *me* judge."

She was sure his compressed lips held back scorching words. But when he said nothing she rose, balancing against the surge of the deck, and left him to sulk.

The moment they docked Xerlanthor hurried off, presumably to the Neck. Zaryas stole a march on him by summoning Xantallon and the Master Magus so urgently they were waiting when she arrived home. When she recounted Xerlanthor's scrying the magi were quite open with their explanation.

"Absolutely unforeseeable," Xantallon said. "When we come to these outcroppings of bedrock I think they're the chief drawback to the whole concept of canals. We're digging so deep now they're a real obstacle. It took every magus in Mishbil all day to crack it—concentrated geomantic earthquakes, and freezing and heating water over the rock to crack it."

"A development that in my judgment justified temporary transfer of personnel," the Master Magus added. "Of course everyone in the dam's corvee slacked off the moment Xerlanthor left town. But I'm afraid that's inevitable when no rigid custom keeps everyone busy."

"He should have conscripted in the traditional way," Xantallon pointed out cheerfully. "There are two sides to every question, of course, my lady. But this 'managing by emulation' idea is nonsense. People obey the proper authorities only to the proper extent. When Xerlanthor demands personal allegiance from the corvee they naturally resent it. They tithe their labor only, not their love. How maddening it must have been to descry all those specially chosen workers taking their ease."

All of a sudden Zaryas was wearily aware of her salt-stiffened clothes and the weight of her travel boots. "I'll be grateful when this is all over," she sighed irrelevantly. "I feel like a juggler spinning too many eggs. Xerlanthor must accede to my judgment on this. But he's convinced it's your fault, and he's not a forgiver."

The Master Magus smiled indulgently at her. "The Order of Magi has survived these little dissensions before," he assured her.

Chapter 9: Olhem

The occasional magian dispute is usually an exciting opportunity for gossip. But now the city had no attention to spare. Through all the fuss the two halves of the dam had slowly grown toward each other across the channel. Now only a narrow slot, perhaps ten paces wide was left between them. The Bilcad forced its cold green torrent through quite silently, for the flow is greatly lessened in winter. And that pressure also seemed to force the riven magi together, pooling their strength against this common foe. For only a fool would call the Dragon tamed. Rather, the current ran with an almost menacing quiet. Beware, the Bilcad murmured. You almost have me, for I sleep. But soon I wake—be ready for that day!

One evening in Olhem Zaryas was feasting some city officials. Custom demanded it, but after so many years it was hard to work up any enthusiasm for the occasion. Thumbprint and its attendant side wagers were the only entertainment. Zaryas did not play. Like an army preparing for a clinching battle, Mishbil had been girding itself for the final push. The work had been so hard all Zaryas wanted to do was sleep. "Thank Viris we need but one dam," she said to her guests. "I haven't the strength to help build another."

Norveth said, "All this fuss is very upsetting. Canals really would have been easier to manage."

He was an ideal second, Zaryas reminded herself. No initiative but any amount of endurance. With a cheerful calm she did not feel she said, "It's too late to change our minds now" She wondered how many times she had said that this past season.

The servers were carrying round trays of fruit—yellow apples a little wrinkled from storage, and pears that were past their best—when the doorkeeper came in. He waited politely for Zaryas to notice him, and then reported, "It's noised all over town, my lady, that the magi have begun to close the gap."

"How exciting!" "In the dark?" "Really!" the guests exclaimed.

"Oh yes indeed," the doorkeeper assured them. "There's a whole line of torches going up the road. No one wants to miss the magery."

"We ought not let them," Norveth declared. "It's unlucky to meddle with magi. Besides, a crowd might get in the way."

Norveth's disapproval always tempted Zaryas to be contrary. This once she felt she could indulge herself. "I'd dearly love to see the feat," she put in. "Let's go up ourselves, and make a party of it!"

The proposal was greeted with enthusiasm. In no time tiles were put away, cloaks donned and oil lamps plucked from their wall holders. So much of the city's life had poured into this venture that everyone felt a proprietary interest.

The Sun had laid himself to rest long ago, and the cold was cruel. Zaryas' embroidered party dress and cloak had no function but the decorative, and she knew the final construction would take all night at least. "Go on ahead," she said. "I'll just run back and get some warmer leggings."

Her house was nearly deserted. With resignation she decided the servants had absconded to the Neck too. She stripped off her necklace and rings and shut them away—outright robbery is rare in Averidan but picking pockets, purloining jewelry, and snatching handkerchiefs is a time-honored calling. She pulled quilted trousers on under her dress, and hesitated over a warm purple cloak that would clash dreadfully with her apricot dress. Then she pounced on the leopard-skin spread on the platform of the bed. The supple hide clung warmly to her thin silk cloak, and the empty furry paws could knot at her throat. She skipped up the steps and down the hall again, with the pale golden leopard-tail bobbing behind her.

It was less than five leagues from the viceroy's house to the Neck, the road paved with oyster shell and lime and shaded by tall sycamores from the summer heats. Ordinarily half a day was necessary to walk it. But from excitement and cold everyone stepped briskly, the torches and lamps shedding sparkles of festive light up either side of the river. "Everyone's going," Zaryas observed. "You'd think it was a holiday or a sacrifice." She was delighted, for Xerlanthor's sake. He loved approval, especially public approval.

"Serve us all right if the rumor was wrong," Norveth grumped. "Whyever did they start at night?"

"I gather the last section will take days to finish anyway," Zaryas said. "So it makes no difference when they begin. Unless there's a magic reason."

The river road now ended where the dam cut it off. Upstream and down both river banks were crowded with people. No one knows how rumor spreads in Averidan, only that it spreads efficiently. Zaryas chose a vantage point atop a low stone wall at the verge. The Bilcad no longer filled its bed. The dark bulk of the dam spanned it, and the narrow torrent looked black as it bubbled out the one opening to reclaim the channel it had dug for itself. On either side of it the newly bared river bottom was full of light cast by tall torches stuck into the sand to light the work.

It was impossible in the wavering glare to pick out Xerlanthor from the other magi. Zaryas narrowed her eyes and peered down. Beside the narrowed flow of water was a clot of red-clad figures. Hydromancy would do the work today, and at Xerlanthor's behest nearly every water-wizard in Averidan was down there. The geo-mancers and herognomers were present only to supply advice and moral support.

Big slabs of granite shielded the unfinished ends of the dam until they could unite. Now the magi gathered on the sand near these slabs. Their numbers were divided evenly on either side of the gap, and the water fanned out to fill its bed between them. No dramatic gestures were made, and the torchlight twinkled steadily on a hundred thick glass wands. But very slowly the fan of chilly green water began to close. The water narrowed and piled up as if invisible banks channeled it in. Soon the torrent flowed dark and tall, wide as the gap and higher than the magi's heads—a wall of living water.

"Now comes the hard part," Zaryas said. Anticipation, and the cold breeze round her ankles, made her hop perilously on the wall. "With nothing but hydromancy they'll hold back the river."

As the gap grew narrower and narrower the Bilcad seemed to notice and take alarm. The torrent squeezed itself through with greater force, splashing everyone to either side. "It's a cold night for a wetting," Norveth observed. But the magi took no notice. The opening inexorably shrank to a size two men's arms could span, then one. It was wide as a door, and at last no wider than a body: a slit that could barely be seen behind the angry river that flung itself out into the night. The water-wall was squeezed so thin now the torches' light shone greenly through it.

Taut with concentration, the hydromants faced
the flow, their hands and wands raised high to
support the water. Between their red-clad backs
Zaryas could make out a row of white blobs—the
faces of the water-wizards on the far side of the
flow, so near that they could have reached through
the water to touch their fellows, if they had had
the energy to spare.

Then some signal was passed. The slit sealed
from top to bottom like a coat being buttoned. In
the sudden quiet a sigh of wonder and delight
escaped from the spectators. The water quivered
in the gap as if it dared not leap forward again.
The magi did not relax. They shuffled round
until they stood shoulder to shoulder, facing the
dam and holding the water up. With the grueling
labor usually devoted to hauling ships into dry-
dock the magi forced the wall of water back
upstream. The dam was very broad at its base, so
that its cross-section was a wide triangle. Reluctantly the wall of water retreated to bare the
granite slabs. They gleamed black and wet in the
torchlight; the leashed river trembled upright
between them like green jelly.

The magi slowly crowded into the gap as they
pushed the water back. Zaryas craned her neck,
but from downstream it was hard to see what
was going on now. "Be careful, my lady," Norveth
warned behind her. "It's a nasty fall down the
bank, if you slip. There won't be much more to
see from here. The construction will be just plain
hard work. We might as well go home."

Many spectators seemed to agree. There was a

general movement homeward; it was too cold to stand outside all night. But Zaryas said, "Non-sense. What's the good of being viceroy if you don't get privileges? I'm going down to get a better look."

She clambered back down off the wall and, leaving her guests to their own devices, hurried further up the road. Her subjects going the other way greeted her politely and with approval. Tasks their princess supervised were done properly. The cold nipped at her cheeks and fingers, but under the fluffy fur rug her body was warm.

Soon she came to the dam. The construction road had been cut from the main road down into the channel below it. At the top foremen in red headbands kept the idly curious out, but let Zaryas pass. The road bent twice to take the slope at a safe angle before leveling out. There the silty riverbed was uneven, gouged down to the underlying rock in spots by the magically manipulated currents. But a walkway of timber had been laid down for convenience.

Dozens of torches brought out the fantastic colors that had been hidden beneath the water: emerald streaked with black pine-pitch, a discarded chicken bone lying in a great smear of orange. To her right the long slope of the dam reared higher than any roof in Mishbil. The unfinished spillway was a dark line down the smooth stone face.

The magi did not notice her until she approached the gap. Then the Master Magus looked up from a scroll and came over to say, "You mustn't go nearer unless it's very urgent, my lady. Any interruption of concentration would be fatal."

"I don't doubt it," Zaryas said. "It's dangerous to meddle with magi. I just want to watch."

"You won't see the like in your lifetime," the Magus said with pride. The river was being forced right out the other side of the gap. When Zaryas peered through she could see its green curve cupping the opening. It looked like a green glass bottle sliced open and set there to hold the water back. The hydromants stood rigid, the red sleeves sliding back from their upraised arms. Behind them Xerlanthor fidgeted. The moment enough room to work was cleared he signaled to Torver, who led forward men armed with shovels.

Mud and sand flew out of the gap, to be scraped into baskets and hauled away. Then the massive stone blocks were rolled up, ten men hauling on ropes while another crew laid log rollers before and took them up after. The various crews were so swift and deft that Zaryas did not have to look for their red headbands and wristlets.

When the first rows of both facing walls were in place chunks of rock and basketfuls of gravelly earth were packed between them and tamped down with stone rollers. Then more blocks were brought up. Even with careful preparations and expert help it was slow work and, as the rising berm hid the hydromants, Zaryas wondered how long they could hold the water away.

"You'll freeze," the Magus prophesied, "unless you come over to the fire and have some tea."

"Just what I was wanting." He led her well downstream of the construction area, and across the puddles and mud that only this evening were the river. A bonfire had been lit on the farther side, and a few camp chairs and work tables stood near. Zaryas sat down and drew up her feet so they could be covered by her fur. She was tired from the long walk, and a little cold from standing so long. It must be near dawn, she thought sleepily. Torch and fire blotted out the stars, so she could not tell the time. She watched the laborers: some stood in the oxcarts to shovel out gravel and rock, while others hauled the laden baskets away and yet others hurried back with the emptied ones to be refilled. She yawned hugely, and tightened the furry paws around her neck.

It was not surprising when Zaryas woke hours later with aching limbs and a crick in her neck from sleeping curled upright. Her back was cozy but her shins and the hands clasped over them felt scorched. Someone must have tended the fire while she slept. Day comes late in winter, but she had slept right through the dawn. The Sun rode high and pale in the crisp cold sky.

Work on the dam was brisk as ever, Zaryas noted with admiration. The gap was more than half filled now. The water on the other side was invisible. Tea utensils were piled carelessly in a basket beside her. She was thirsty, and certainly the magi might like a cup too. A stoneware kettle hung on an extending hook near the fire. Prudently she lifted the lid. "Empty," she said aloud in satisfied tones. A lucky thing she had not assumed it was full—heating an empty kettle would shatter it—but magi are notoriously lax housekeepers. She emptied the basket, searching for a water-flask, but found none. Of course with the river flowing no one had needed a flask. However, now she was reluctant to dip water from the silty standing pools in mid-channel. "I suppose the nearest well is leagues away," she grumbled, remembering how the Neck area had been cleared. A river's worth of water was on the other side of the dam, but she could not reach it. Or could she?

The granite-paved face of the dam sloped temptingly up beside her. The stones had not been given their final smoothing yet—her shoes would not slip. Warily she approached the dam, half expecting Xerlanthor to shout objections. But he must have been busy in the gap. The rise was shallow as a staircase, the ascent easy.

The top of the dam was flat and broad as a street. A finishing pavement would someday be laid, but now she had to walk carefully on the rough gravel lest she turn an ankle. When complete the dam would span the channel like a bridge. She peered over the other side. The slope that had seemed so easy to scale on the downstream side looked ominous footed in water. The little lake was hardly bigger than the river channel yet, but she knew soon the water would back up and rise to the top of the dam. The sullen pool was unmoving, green-brown from silt and vegetation. She wrinkled her nose at it.

To her right a bubble of air protruded upstream. The magi had held the river from the
gap all this time. On either edge of the gap timbers and pulleys were set up, to lift loads up.
The work gangs that hauled on the ropes rested
squatting while their foreman watched for sig-
nals from below. They were unsurprised to see
Zaryas, well knowing she turned up unexpectedly to see if work was going properly. Zaryas
passed politely between them and leaned over
the raw edge of the dam.

She was just in time to glimpse a rare lull in
construction activity. Between the slope of the
new segment and the curving wall of water the
hydromants still stood rigid. For a moment she
could not fathom why work had stopped. Then
she saw the night's labor had raised the last
section of the dam above the water line. At last
the hydromants could relax their power, and let
the water take its natural level. But first they
had to lift, or be lifted up and out of the way.

"For the other sections it was easy," the foreman at her elbow remarked. "The magi just slid
sideways out from under the water. But now—"
He shook his head.

"Surely Xerlanthor has thought of something,"
Zaryas said. Even as she spoke, the line of
hydromants shifted. Perhaps half a dozen of them
relaxed and stepped out of the line of red backs.
Those remaining crowded together to continue
their steady magical support. Unless Xerlanthor
planned some novel stratagem the entire weight

of water would soon be borne by a very few magi. "That's terribly risky!" Zaryas exclaimed.

"My lord Xerlanthor sanctioned it," the foreman defended. "He said there's no other way." He thought for a moment and added, "According to plaiv every great construction claims lives."

"I don't believe it," Zaryas said. "Xerlanthor would never deliberately sacrifice anyone." But her words rang hollow when she surveyed the work site below. The circle of magi closed in as hydromants were subtracted. Those released scrambled wearily up the long new-laid slope to join the crowd of magi at the top.

At last only three water-wizards held back the eager water. It was hard to recognize anyone from this angle, but Zaryas thought the thinnest one was Xantallon. The multiplied strain, on top of a long night's hydromantic labor, made the three sway where they stood at the foot of the dam. "They can't keep that up," Zaryas worried. "The water's too heavy for three." It occurred to her that here was an ideal way to get rid of a hydromant. Was Xerlanthor capable of such cunning? She discovered she did not know.

The magi on top were clustering at the very verge. Some sat thigh to thigh on the raw edges of the topmost stones, while others leaned over their shoulders. With the awkward strained concentration of one climbing a staircase on stilts they exerted their water-magic again. The water-wall was at least fifteen paces away. It was impossible they could hold it back, at that distance, for more than a moment or two.

But the instant their colleagues above took control, the three magi below turned and ran. The wall of turbid water cast a cold green shadow up the slope. They raced as if that shadow could grab their ankles and hold them back. "They'll do it!" the foreman exclaimed.

"I knew Xerlanthor could," Zaryas said, sighing with relief.

The wall of water wavered. Then it crumpled. The green wall trembled and fell forward, first down to the sands and then up in foaming fury, reaching for the heels of its fleeing tyrants.

At that very instant the slowest magus slipped. He tumbled flat on his face, and frantically lurched upright again. But it was too late. The froth surged up and over him, and swallowed him up.

"The rope!" Zaryas cried. "Lower the rope!" Everyone lunged for the pulley release. A thick bronze hook weighted the line. The pulleys whined in protest as the hook plummeted down. The two magi remaining pelted up unseeing, while their brethren at the top sat stunned. Only when the angry water leaped up and drenched them all did they snatch to secure the two survivors.

"I don't see him," Zaryas said, shading her eyes against the light. No red robe gleamed through the green-brown murk. "Could the impact have stunned him?" The rope dangled slack, pushed to and fro by the diminishing waves. The magi splashed down into the cold water, calling. Those with the skill brushed the water aside, digging shallow dimples into the aloof surface.

Others probed with staff and hands. But the river kept its countenance.

"He's gone," the foreman said. "And I'll bet it wasn't the impact. It was the Dragon." The work crew murmured agreement. Numb with shock Zaryas did not object when they began removing rings and searching in belt pouches. Perhaps the folk wisdom was right after all. When the pathetic little offerings tinkled down the stone slope into the water the weary magi glanced up in annoyance. "Superstition," she thought she heard someone scold, but they were too far below, and the breeze pushed their words away.

Her companions took no notice. "It isn't enough," the foreman said. "We need more." With a start Zaryas noticed they were all peering discreetly sideways at her. The other side of reality seemed fearfully close—that realm where myth can rise up living from sleep to catch one down, where things heard and half-believed in plaiv and legend suddenly demand homage. She rubbed her bare wrists and fingers. She had left every valuable at home. Then she pulled the leopardskin off. Wordlessly the work crew helped her knot up the supple fur and weight it down with stones. She needed their help too to swing the bundle out in a long arc to fall into deep water. The resounding splash startled everyone below. The chill bit through her silken blouse and robe now, and Zaryas shivered. Let that be enough, she silently begged the Dragon.

Chapter 10: The Rest of Winter, and Spring

Perhaps somewhere in the world there are folk who finish works with style. The Shan prefer to taper off, spinning out the finishing touches because they never quite decide when a given project is complete. Long after the dam was done Xerlanthor pottered back and forth over the newly spanned channel, adjusting the final stone paving or supervising the installation of the great bronze sluice-gates. The hydromants returned to planning canals, and the exhausted corvee gratefully went home. Only a half-dozen foremen lingered to help tidy up.

As Olnep faded, even Xerlanthor could no longer pretend to be busy. Zaryas included him in her meetings and sessions so that he could learn government and so prepare for married life. But often he slipped away, spending long hours roaming round the city until almost against his will he was drawn farther and farther west, upriver past the farms and the network of canals, to the Neck. There the brown water was very slowly accumulating behind the dam. The true test would come in Spring when it must hold back a winter's worth of snow-melt. For that final proof Xerlanthor had to wait with whatever patience he could muster.

Dimly Zaryas sensed the suspense that tormented him. What had been omitted? What had not been considered? It was too late to alter anything, but the mocking doubts remained. The suspense was made crueler by his relative idleness, and the exhausted indifference of the people. No ceremony marked the ending of the work as they had the beginning. Hardly anyone congratulated the magi on their job—it would be imprudent, if not downright unlucky, to anticipate ultimate success. "And I'd thought I'd be a hero," Xerlanthor complained, only half joking.

"You will be, give it time," Zaryas said. But she knew his thought—that it was a failure of love for him.

The flatness of anticlimax pervaded the city, and in planning the spring sowing the Council was almost sullen. "It's too late to do anything but back our luck," Zaryas said to them. "We must assume the canals will flow properly with water next season. Every field must be sown for early barley in the next few weeks."

"But what if the canals don't?" a farmer demanded. He glanced toward the corner where Xerlanthor sat, but there was no angry rebuttal.

Zaryas refused to admit the possibility. "If they do, the crop should be stupendous," she said. In the face of her serene confidence even the most doubtful took heart.

Another landowner rose to speak. "It's not that we don't trust you, my lady. Or the magi's calculations, or the labor of our own hands either. But oughtn't we hold back a little seed-grain just in case?"

"In case of what? We need—no, we must have—a big harvest," Zaryas pointed out. "Mishbil's belly has been filled by towns and districts all Averidan over. Our credit is strained to the limit. The time for timidity is past, messirs. We must wager all."

No further objections were voiced, but Zaryas could feel the undertow of mulish reluctance urging her along, strong as the outgoing tide. There is in rulership a time to give way—or at least appear to. "However," she added as if it had just occurred to her, "perhaps it would be as well to continue the canal remodeling."

"It would be a pity to idle away these cool winter months."

"It can do no harm," several councillors chimed in, and so it was decided.

She was pleased with her cunning, and when the Council had bowed and withdrawn crowed, "Didn't I manage that beautifully?"

But Xerlanthor's seat was empty. So that was why he had seemed so meek! Annoyed, she realized he must have slipped out quite early on. She trotted out the private door in search, and glimpsed him on the terrace.

Tart words trembled on her tongue as she approached him. But she saw he was leaning on the balustrade, staring west, and instead remarked gently, "You can't see the Neck from here."

He started, and then said, "No, I suppose not."

"You should try it from the little balcony, though I think the roofs around are too high." The thin, late-morning sunlight gilded the white-tile roofs but lent only mild warmth. Flecks of mist like beaten egg white floated in the seaward sky, and the air was cool and moist. Old Winter was nominally lord over Mishbil, but the hand of Spring was already everywhere. Zaryas said, "I shouldn't worry about the dam if I were you. Everyone did their very best. Only time will tell if the best was sufficient."

"I'm not worrying about that," he said irritably. "My plans and calculations are correct, I'm absolutely confident of it—as far as they went. But what if there's something else?"

A chilly breeze seemed to trickle down Zaryas' back. "What?"

"If I knew I could deal with it," he sighed. "It must be some other factor, something quite outside the hydraulic system. Beyond the neat circle of canals and river and dam."

For a moment a cold foreboding weighed down her tongue. The unknown and therefore dreadful future lurked round some dark corner before her, waiting. Then common sense reasserted itself. "That's what happens when you want something too much," she declared. "If the sky doesn't tumble before your desire is achieved, the earth might open up. I said so, that first evening, remember?"

His somber face lightened as he smiled. "Surely I do," he said. A thick plait of her hair hung down over the balustrade, and he took it up gently to examine the silver-wire clasp that fastened it. That drew her closer, and she leaned her head against him for an instant, completely happy.

The moment passed. Three donkeys laden with pottery packed in straw went by on the farther road, and the boy driver waved at them. Zaryas waved back, but Xerlanthor did not move. "You must not think hardly of my folk," she told him. "If they had the arts of diplomacy they wouldn't be the farmers and fishers and merchants they are."

"They dislike me," Xerlanthor said with some bitterness. "They always have, though for love of you they pretended otherwise."

"Not at all. You must not expect to win their affections with one large gift, impressive though it might be. Little by little is the way—a steady regard."

"I've limited that regard all my life," he said, "to magery. And then I met you. Don't let's stretch my affections too quickly yet." With a grave, courtly gesture he saluted her. "You are my sanity, Zaryas. I must make very sure never to lose you."

"This summer," she promised.

The spring sowing proceeded without further incident. Zaryas spent long days striding up and down flat brown fields, to lend the enterprise her explicit endorsement. Also, she wanted to be certain the precious seed was sown properly.

Except for those who had pressing magic duties elsewhere the magi lingered in Mishbil. They were of course professionally interested in how the dam would bear up in its first season. As she manipulated scanty food supplies Zaryas often secretly wished they would depart. But the traditions of official hospitality did not allow her to even ask questions about exciting projects elsewhere.

But on the last day of Olnep the Master Magus himself sought her out. She was visiting a windy and distant farm-holding near the sea, one of those family settlements that combine fishing with farming. Already thin green leaves were veiling the wild sea-plum thickets. The worried farmer showed her the tracks of sand-leopard cubs beside the canal. When out of the corner of her eye Zaryas saw the Master Magus lifting toward them, far over the flat bare fields, she took him for a bird. There were many that day riding the blue spring sky.

"Princess!" he called. His thin old voice sounded exactly like a bird's whistle. "News!"

The Master Magus especially was far too important to run minor errands. Zaryas took a deep breath as the Magus carefully eased himself to earth. "I must return to the capital," he said, panting. "Shan Varim King has died."

Zaryas could not speak. The farmer, who had inquisitively lingered within earshot, cried, "May the White Queen receive him! How did it happen?"

"Varim was old," the Magus replied briefly. "The Collegium of Counsellors, which I head, must meet to choose a new King," he added to Zaryas.

"I shall initiate mourning in Mishbil immediately," Zaryas said. All of a sudden her throat ached with tears. "Varim was King all my life. It's like being told the Dragon spread his wings and flew off. May he journey safe to the Deadlands."

"I have seen three Kings of the Shan," the Magus said heavily. "Offer, my dear, that we may once again choose a King rightly. And—" He hesitated and then continued, "It weighs on me, though, that I won't be here."

"Nonsense," Zaryas said. "Don't worry about us, all will be well here. You've got enough on your plate as it is."

There was time to say little more. Many of the magi departed with their Master, for at such times there is need all Averidan over for familiar authorities and Orders. In Mishbil, banners of coarse mourning black were hung from every window and thin black streamers tied to cattle-yokes and the prows of ships. All the King's representatives, from Zaryas down to the most minor bureaucrats, wore loose black linen surcoats over their everyday clothes. At the official sacrifice on behalf of the Collegium, the worthies of Mishbil looked like a flock of crows. Parties, picnics, and festivals were banned, not that anyone in Mishbil had the time or provisions for them anyway.

For when the Shan King passes, his subjects lose more than a ruler. The King bridges the gap between past and present, linking the Shan with their fathers and forefathers. Who else can judge what tradition and custom truly are except the Shan King? Until a new monarch is chosen and crowned Averidan drifts, helpless as a ship without a rudder. Zaryas could not shake the uneasy feeling that she now ruled alone. There was no Shan King behind her to advise or amend now, if she lost confidence or failed in any way.

"But how does the Collegium choose the next Shan King?" Xerlanthor asked her once.

"You ought to know more than I," Zaryas said. "Your Master heads the Collegium. But don't tell me about it. Everyone knows it's an arcane and hidden rite, not at all for common inquiry."

"It's nothing to be shy about," he declared. "Merely a political process. I wonder who it'll be."

Though sowing was nearly done there was plenty to do. The pearl-fishing season opened without its usual festival but with rather more than the usual number of sacrifices to Ennelith for calm seas and safe sailing. Now it was really spring ships from other countries, faraway Oorsevesh and Colb in the south, put into harbor for provisions and water, and sometimes to hire Viridese pilots for the sail north through the treacherous shoals to the City. Zaryas graciously received these foreigners and spent happy hours with Xerlanthor examining their trade-goods—greasy green-black ivory in chunks tall as a man,

jars of oil-fruit to be processed into nard, black
and yellow carpets reeking of odd perfumes and
spirally embroidered in red thread with the names
of strange devils.

All this time with almost imperceptible slow-
ness water collected behind the dam. The Spring
that was awakening seeds planted in the valley
crept inland, melting mountain snows and soft-
ening cold weather with rain in the distant up-
lands. The Bilcad, spine of the Dragon, sustainer
of Mishbil, shed its winter torpor and swelled
silver in its bed again. When Zaryas went with
Xerlanthor to the Neck she could see from week
to week the mud-colored pool mounting. First it
grew high enough to fill the span between the
two bluffs. Then as the pool spread it crept up to
fill the canals, invading land farther and farther
upstream.

In mid-Ynbas when the first barley seed came
up everyone was absurdly pleased. Suddenly red
headbands and wristlets became quite fashion-
able again. Xerlanthor received several requests
for house-geomancy, which he did not deal in at
all. "Quackery!" he exclaimed. "Once the house
is built the influence of the earth currents on it
is forever set. No rearrangement of furniture or
window-hangings can alter it!"

"That's not what people *believe*," Zaryas argued. "And it would look so well. Oblige a few
silly people; go and tell them to move their beds
away from the windows. Everyone in town will
think you're wonderful. Remember what I said,
about a steady regard?"

"Serve them right if I prescribe expensive re-building," he grumbled, but conceded the point.

No one was more delighted with the barley than Zaryas. "I couldn't be prouder if I'd sown every field myself," she told Xerlanthor one day. "Do you think we've pulled it off?"

From where they stood on the dam's broad top a delicate pale green mist could be seen hovering over the bare fields to the northeast and southeast. Each individual new blade of barley was short and fine as an eyebrow hair, but from a distance the hundreds of sprouted grains could be perceived clearly. Best of all, the fields watered by the newly filled canals were plainly greener and lusher than the ones farther out. "Wait a few months," Xerlanthor boasted. "Grain must have water to set seed. By that time all the canals will be restored to service. The harvest should be phenomenal."

"And will Xantallon get some of the credit for that?" Zaryas teased him.

"Whyever for?" Xerlanthor said. "What would his work be but for mine?"

"Oh, you're impossible," Zaryas laughed. It was easy to make light of the proud words. The tide of Spring, of renewed life and luck, was rising. Zaryas was certain deep in herself of her excellent fortune, even before she called on the Mistress.

Chapter 11: Mid-Ynnem

In common with the rest of her race Zaryas had complete confidence in the wishes granted at the Temple of the Sun. So she was calm as she wended her way past the great seashell gate of the Sodality of Ennelith, and through the tiny interlocking courtyards. No one demanded to know her business, or interefered with her progress in any way, though the impression of unraveling a bewildering maze, or exploring some secret inner realm, was very strong. No locks are put into the doors of the Sodality, for Ennelth is strong enough to guard her own. But Zaryas did not hesitate. The Goddess would know her by now, since she had called on the Mistress before.

The inmost cypresswood door was ajar. Zaryas tapped politely on it before peering in. The Mistress was seated at a desk near a wide window. Outside a green-blue sea curled endlessly up the gravelly beach, and two seagulls quarreled over a bit of stale bread.

The Mistress rose and smiled in welcome. "Princess."

Zaryas took the proffered hand. "I'm here personally, Mistress, not on Mishbil's affairs."

"Indeed!" The Mistress still held Zaryas' hand between her own warm palms. "You're with child!"

With a blush Zaryas pulled her hand free. "Are you sure? You can tell by my touch?"

"I represent the Goddess' power," the Mistress reminded her. "Did our potions fail you?"

"Not at all," Zaryas said. "Xerlanthor forbade them, he said he is unable to father children. I wished for them anyway, at the Sun Temple, and also sacrificed to Ennelith. Is it irreverent to ask if I benefit from a miracle?"

This mistress considered the question carefully before replying, "Ennelith has immutable rules, that no persuasion will swerve. Experiences like yours aren't unheard of, but they result from some special operation of the Goddess' laws, not a specific dispensation of them. Did Xerlanthor ever confide to you a reason for his infertility?"

"I didn't know there was one," Zaryas said. "Doesn't it just happen?"

"Oh, no, there is always a cause." The Mistress consulted many scrolls from the racks lining the walls of the room while an acolyte in pale blue linen poured tea for Zaryas. The seagulls had eaten the bread and were now disputing a clump of jetsam near the tide-line. At last the Mistress said, "There are many reasons in our records why a man might not father children. This might fit your case. 'When the male suffers from a thinness of his seed, he may only sire children rarely, after persistent attempts with one partner.' "

The mechanics of the miracle did not interest Zaryas at all. It was more exciting to look forward to Xerlanthor's surprise and delight. "I shall tell him myself first," she decided, "but not the rest of Mishbil. There's no need to disclose all these details."

"That's the proper way," the Mistress agreed, for the custom is to announce births, not conception. With a swoop of silken sleeves she enfolded Zaryas in a congratulatory embrace. "Ennelith's blessings on you both—or should I say, all three of you?"

"I'll come back with an offering very soon," Zaryas said, returning the hug. A genial communion with all mothers, all the fruitful and giving forces of nature, filled her as she took her leave. How pleasant and appropriate it would be to bear a child, and just around harvest time, too. She felt a healthy appetite for food and exercise. Her braids bobbed with the speed of her step as she danced out a side entrance onto the beach road. To her mild surprise the afternoon did not reflect her lightheartedness. The stony beach was dull, and the sea sullen for lack of sunlight. The gulls were gone. She craned her neck to look at the Sun. Long low clouds were scudding up from the west, blotting out the light. That was unusual in Mishbil at any time of the year, but not alarming. Still, it would be best to get home. Smugly, she told herself it was a duty to take good care of herself now.

By the time she had walked down the beach to where the Bilcad ran into the sea the overcast cloaked the sky from east to west. The river-quays seethed with uneasy sailors and merchants, out to see the strange weather and speculate about its significance. "What does it mean, princess?" a candy vendor asked her.

"We must ask the herognomers," Zaryas replied. "I've never seen the like."

"Neither have I," the vendor said. "And I'm sixty, come next Olbas."

"If this were the northern or western provinces," a sailor remarked, "I'd say it looked like rain. But it can't be."

The unheard-of clouds hung over the city until dusk hid them from view. Nervously Zaryas ordered sacrifices made to every deity and supernatural guardian, and consulted weather-wise seamen and herognomers. "It's simply clouds," the air-wizards reported. "The air-currents have shifted east of us, drawing the weather after them."

"Why?" Zaryas demanded.

"They were warmed by the ocean currents," the herognomers said. Impatiently Zaryas would have asked why the ocean currents had suddenly decided to be warm, but the Harbor Master interrupted with a question about how this would affect fishing, and so she forgot the query.

Chapter 11: 20 Ynnem

Very early next morning, while Mishbil still slept, the rain began to fall. Round gleaming drops large and heavy as ripened grapes tinkled and clattered intermittently on sandy earth and baked-clay roof tiles. Then with a rush and a roar the heavens opened and poured down their juices. Thornbushes, unaccustomed to such epiphanies, sagged down over their sodden roots. The gutters that ran down every street ran now with more than street-cleaning water. Every unmended roof or misaligned drain joyously proclaimed its defect, usually by dropping cold water down necks or into linen closets.

Zaryas was dreaming the Eye Pool had turned into a fountain overnight, drenching everyone in the marketplace, when Xerlanthor shook her awake. "It's raining," he announced.

"It can't be. Where was it last year, when we needed extra water?" She yawned. The unusual darkness of cloud had made her oversleep.

"It hasn't rained in Mishbil in living memory. We should enjoy it while we can."

Somewhere in the house there must have been a leak, for an irregular patch of dampness was spreading across the plaster ceiling. Like all houses in Mishbil, this one was made of mud-brick, plastered and painted. A strange moist odor pervaded the air, the smell of wet earth, wet plaster, wet clothing, wet tiles, wet wood, wet shoes. The constant murmur of falling droplets was very odd and a little disturbing. "It's positively indecent," Zaryas declared as she dressed. "All this water for free, for no effort at all. If it rained here every day no one would work on canals or dams."

"If it rained here every day," Xerlanthor said, "they wouldn't be necessary."

At the heaviness of his tone her heart almost seemed to stop beating. "Will your dam hold up under all this water?"

He was slow to reply. "I don't know," he said at last. "Let's hope it doesn't rain too long."

"I can't believe it will," Zaryas said. They wrapped up in cloaks and went out to see the strange phenomenon. Mishbil looked utterly foreign. Streets and buildings were dark and wet. Passersby huddled under garments or roundels of thin-beaten greenish copper—gongs taken off their stands. Vapor rose from the earth, and the Eye Pool quivered with dancing drops.

The steady downpour soaked through a linen cloak almost instantly. "We might as well accept being wet," Xerlanthor said. He let his sodden cloak fall and took off his cap. The rain plastered his hair in black clumps down his forehead, and dripped steadily off his nose. He paced along with a jaunty air as if he felt superior to merely physical elements. That made her laugh.

"You can't be comfortable," Zaryas said. "At least with a cloak one makes the gesture." For a while it was amusing to splash along hand in hand, wet to the skin, the water squelching out of their shoes. A deliberate merriment possessed them, a conscious delighting in the present moment. Zaryas pretended not to notice when Xerlanthor guided their steps steadily westward, toward the Neck.

But their progress became slower and slower. First the water was sole-deep, then ankle-deep. The gutters overflowed in every street, so that lanes became rivers and roads torrents. Very soon they had to wade, stubbing their toes on hidden kerbstones and water-borne trash. The ways seemed curiously rough, perhaps because they could not see. Xerlanthor pointed at a dead rat bobbing past and panted, "Cellars must be flooding all over town."

It had never occurred to Zaryas that rain could kill. "Is it safe to be out in this?" she asked.

"I want to see the dam," he admitted at last. "But you needn't come along."

"No, I can keep up."

It was a little better west of the city center, where the waters were not channeled by buildings. The tall sycamores along the road seemed to droop their boughs into the water. Houses presided helplessly over flowing sheets of water that had once been gardens or courtyards. The dry sandy soil could not retain the runoff. Xerlanthor wiped his face and peered for a glimpse of the river, but the streaming rain hid everything.

There was no doubt now the road was washing away. Zaryas stepped again and again into deep potholes. Every time the jolt seemed to loosen her teeth. Gravel and sand scoured past her calves. "Let's stop and rest a bit," Xerlanthor suggested.

It was good to pause beneath one of the roadside sycamores. Gratefully they leaned against the gleaming wet bark where the new broad leaves gave a little shelter. Zaryas bent to rinse out accumulated grit from her shoes. "I'll have the Director of Roadworks lapidated," she declared.

"There isn't a road in Averidan built to take this," Xerlanthor replied. "Nor a roof, nor a house. This is no ordinary rain. It's a cataclysm."

Zaryas would not have believed clouds could hold so much water. If anything the rain was pelting down even harder. The dirty water that swirled past seemed only a little less close than the cascade from the sky. Even in the tree's scant shelter the numbing, bewildering power of it was like stepping under a waterfall. "I must go back," she said at last. "If this is no ordinary storm I must be where my people can find me."

"You might have said so before," Xerlanthor exclaimed. "We've come at least a league and a half. Now I'll have to take the time to help you home."

"It's my duty to be there," she defended.

"Well, for that matter, my duty is at the dam."

Now they had stopped walking Zaryas had

time to realize how tired she was. The exercise
had been warming at first but now in her soaked
tunic she was shivering. Far more sharply than
she had intended to she retorted: "If it holds, it
holds, there's nothing you can accomplish by being
there." Articulating their unspoken fear seemed
to give it power. Realizing that she sounded like
a child frightened to go to bed alone she said,
"I'm perfectly capable of walking a league home
myself."

She saw the anger harden his mouth. She had
never provoked it before. "Don't be a fool," he
snapped. "In this?" He would have gone on, with
untold unforgivable words. But in a different
tone he interrupted himself. "Is it my imagination, or is this tree *moving*?"

Startled, Zaryas looked up. It was hard to say,
what with the water swirling round their legs
and the fat cold drops descending on their heads.
But she thought there was indeed a slight seasicky
motion to either the invisible earth beneath her
feet or the living wood at her back. "Or maybe
it's us," she suggested. "You don't feel feverish,
do you?"

Suddenly his face seemed to blanch. She tried
to blink the steady rain out of her eyes and see
better. With harsh alarm he cried, "Run!"

The jerk he gave her arm nearly wrenched it
from her shoulder. "What is it?" she gasped as
she splashed stumbling after him. A rending,
sucking sound behind them obliterated any reply
he might have made. With a crash that sprayed
dirty water up all around them the sycamore

toppled down across the roadway. The supporting earth had been eroded away from its roots.

Like the avenging claws of a dragon the threshing boughs caught her. Zaryas struggled in vain. The weight of the tree as it settled on its side bore her down, down, farther than she thought possible. The water seemed fathoms deep. The cold flood clutched at her garments, forced itself into her mouth and eyes. The clumsy magus had died this way. She would drown, held down in the dark, hidden under the roiling water, and when the flood receded her bloated body would be left hanging on the branches of the dead sycamore like some untimely fruit.

Terror stripped away all her mental vestments. As her body failed her she could have bared imaginary teeth at death, like a trapped rat. The fiery determination to live consumed even thought for Xerlanthor. Locked in her struggle it did not occur to her that he also might be drowning in the cold dark.

Then the tangle of branches seemed to relent. The weight across her body eased. It was raining so hard she did not realize at first that her head had broken through the surface. Her first gasp for air sounded like a sob in her ringing ears. She had not given in. She was alive.

Xerlanthor was splashing in the waist-deep torrent beside her. With frantic haste he tore her free, as if the tree might change its mind. "I thought I'd lost you," he gasped, crushing her to his wet chest. "Thank Viris I had the strength to roll the tree a little."

"So it was you." Reaction made her limp and a little dizzy. The warm solidity of his shoulder was comforting but not quite real. The sweet, moist air in her lungs was all she had ever wanted, and the deluge, the dam, all receded into insignificance. With an effort she remembered her manners. "Thank you. You saved my life."

"Are you hurt?" He explored her back and limbs with hands that were abrupt with anxiety. She submitted with such uncharacteristic patience that he became alarmed. "Did you hit your head?"

"No," she panted. "But I'm going to be sick." The water she had had to choke down lay like a slab of ice on her stomach. She leaned over his supporting arm to spew it up.

When she was done he said, "Just relax, I'm going to lift us home."

Feebly she protested, "Is that safe, in this storm?"

"Not really. But I've had some practice." She could not see if he was smiling. She made no further objection as he clasped her tightly against him. The surging water sank away, and they were flying through the downpour, no longer bound to earth. The sky took them in. Yet even here the storm was cruel. The wind cut right through Zaryas' wet clothes, and lashed icy rain at her face. It was more like swimming than flying. She burrowed deeper into Xerlanthor's arms and closed her eyes.

When she opened them again they were already hovering over the city. It was so far below she felt no sense of actuality at all. Like a map-tray, Mishbil was spread neatly below their feet. All the streets were threaded with silver water, and the Eye Pool had overflowed. She could almost touch the lowering ceiling of cloud above their heads. Through rifts in the rain-curtain they could sometimes see leagues away.

She felt the sudden tension in the arms that encircled her before he spoke. "There, did you see that?" Xerlanthor cried. "It must be the lake!"

She gasped at the sight of it. Overnight the reluctant little lake had gorged fat on rain and runoff. Pale and gross, it had invaded farmsteads and gullies, pressed itself right up to the lip of Xerlanthor's dam. The fury of the storm was less cold than the sudden dread that the lake might run over.

Without warning they began to fall, in the swift yet controlled stoop of a hawk dropping on its prey. The swollen Eye Pool rapidly expanded below Zaryas' feet. Only when Xerlanthor set them down on her private little balcony did she grasp his intention. "You're going back to the Neck?"

"Yes." The strain of lifting through the storm made his chilly hands tremble a little as he closed them over hers. "Send workers, as many as you can find, the magi, and especially my foremen. We'll try sandbags."

"Oh, my dearest—" She hugged him. For a brief instant he leaned his head on her shoulder as if the burden was too great for him. Then he freed himself and stepped back. Without further words he lifted, and the rain took him in.

Her fingers were clumsy with cold as Zaryas pried up the trap door. The drip from her soaked clothing ran down before her and made the narrow stair slippery. As soon as she descended to the hall she ran, tripping over her broken shoes, from her part of the house to the main section. When she burst into the arched passage a few dozen bureaucrats were watching the downpour from its shelter.

"Princess, it's *raining*," the senior chamberlain greeted her.

"I'm well aware of it," Zaryas snapped. "You, run to the guest wing and tell the magi to hurry to the Neck. Say that the dam's spillways can't handle this flood. You three, find the roster of Xerlanthor's foremen and divide it among you. Find them all and send them to the Neck. And you, chamberlain, gather together the guardsmen, all the city workers who came to work today. Everyone in my employ is to hurry to the Neck to fill sandbags. I'll give you a requisition, you can pick up the sacks from the grain dealers."

"But we'll get wet," the unfortunate chamberlain protested.

"You'll all get a lot wetter very soon!" Zaryas flashed back. "Don't you understand? If the dam overflows, here we all are, right in the path of the torrent!"

They ran, then. Zaryas debated with herself whether to order the evacuation of the city. Surely it would suffice to have the people climb to the rooftops? But she could not risk it. The unbaked mud-brick that most of Mishbil was made of could never withstand long wetting. She considered how to mobilize an entire city population to hurry several miles in the pouring rain. There was no provision in Mishbil for sudden disaster, no system of general warning. Bitterly she contemplated the reasons for that appalling oversight. The last war in Viridese territory had been fought eight hundred years ago, and then the Shan had lost. From then until now they had never needed vigilance. There was not even an army garrison in Mishbil. The Shan King maintained a token force at the capital only for the sake of tradition. And anyway, there was no Shan King now.

Then Zaryas knew where to obtain ready help and obedient hands. As fast as she could she slogged through the rain-lashed streets to Ennelith's temple. By the mercy of the Goddess the Mistress herself was at the great seashell gate, watching the storm from its shelter. Her blue-clad assistants cried out in dismay at the sight of Zaryas' muddy clothes and broken, soaking shoes. "Call up the Sodality," Zaryas panted to the Mistress. "We must evacuate Mishbil immediately."

The acolytes and novices burst out in shrill questions and exclamations, but the Mistress was serene. "Where shall the populace flee to?"

Zaryas did not know. "To high ground," she said. "Either north or south of the Bilcad channel will do. Knock on every door, warn each household to flee."

The Mistress left the dispatching of her women

to her seconds and guided Zaryas to a bench. "Sit and rest," she urged in a low voice. "You look frightful, you must consider your condition."

For a moment Zaryas was tempted to obey. Her cold hands and feet seemed to have no blood in them at all. Their skin was pale as a fish's belly, and wrinkled from the day's wettings. She trembled with weariness, and longed for a cup of hot tea.

But a demon of fear would not let Zaryas rest. The child within her was not immediate, but distant as next year's harvest. "Food," she remembered. "We must not lose all our food stores to the floods. Let someone go to warn the granaries." Someone lent her a pair of sandals, and she laced them on.

"I'll go to the granaries," the Mistress promised.

"And we'll need bonesetters, herbals," Zaryas continued. When she stepped out the gate the rain hardly seemed cold anymore to her wet body. Already the women of the Sodality were hurrying out the gate, holding their blue cloaks over their heads as they splashed away. As she and the Mistress hurried out along the river road Zaryas remembered she had not warned the archivists to secure the genealogical records. But surely their ancestors' living descendants were more important—

"Look!" The Mistress shrieked and pointed. To their right a long curve in the Bilcad allowed a view upstream. A curl of foam poured into the river just where distance and rain veiled it. It roared downstream faster than a man could run.

And the sound, the deep gnashing thunder of
enraged water, swept ahead—the bellow of the
Dragon of Mishbil. Zaryas stared, unable to grasp
the significance of this new peril. But the Mistress cried, "That isn't overflow! The dam must
have burst under the strain! Quickly—have you
your knife?"

The Mistress drew a short table dagger from
her belt and ran to the road's edge. Zaryas hastened after as the Mistress leaped off the stone
parapet. Below, the narrow pebble beach already
was drowned deep in the gurgling brown river.
Boatmen who cannot afford proper boathouses
drag their dinghys and punts up onto the gravel
and tie them to the wall below the road. Now
those vessels bobbed on the rising tide, straining
at their moorings. The Bilcad was nearly over-
flowing.

Her skirts trailed in a rowboat's dirty bilge,
the Mistress hacked at its ropes. The boat drifted
free, listing a little from its ballast of rainwater.
The Mistress half leaped, half-fell into the next
barge, and staggered up to cut it loose also.

Zaryas scrambled off the parapet into a dinghy. When the flood came only boats would be
able to traverse the streets of Mishbil. If these
were not cut free to float on the surge they would
founder. The thick hempen ropes were slimy
and wet. It was hard to balance against the boat's
jerk. But when the Mistress held the rope taut it
went a little faster. Zaryas sawed at it with her
bigger blade.

Of course it was impossible. All of a sudden

the dinghy reared upward like a wounded bird.
The river climbed up over the gunwale and
poured into Zaryas' lap. The Mistress clutched
wildly at Zaryas' outstretched hand, missed, and
fell overboard. With feverish haste Zaryas slashed
the dinghy free before it was overwhelmed. She
dared waste no time to bail, though it wallowed
almost full of water. "Mistress!" she screamed.
"Mistress!" Only the rush of water and the roar
of falling rain answered her.

The current would soon capsize the boat unless she turned it. There were no paddles, but a
barge-pole was wedged up between two submerged
boats and she grabbed it. Clumsily Zaryas pointed
the prow downstream, and then set to with the
earthenware bailer. Her face was wet, but not,
she hoped, with tears. She had no time to cry
now. There was too much to do.

Zaryas found she could pole right up over the
embankment. The Dragon had reclaimed Mishbil,
and ran chest-deep down what had once been
the road. The whirling currents sucked down
pedestrians and the scour of water undermined
house foundations. Many who climbed to an upper story and thought themselves safe died when
their walls collapsed. The rains peeled tiles from
rooves, plaster from mud-brick, earth from rock.
The city seemed to be sinking, melting into the
waters.

A thick numbing blanket muffled her emotions. Zaryas did not try to fight it. The long
habits of efficiency now carried her forward un-
wavering. She fished out a drowned beggar, and

gave him the pole while she helped a young father with three children and their grandmother
into the dinghy. Then she steered the laden boat
past the mounds of waterlogged rubble to what
had once been a guild-hall—the Glassblowers,
she noticed distantly. The walls had sagged and
brought the roof down. But the timbers had been
soundly bolted together, and the roof lay more or
less in one piece in the middle of the square.
"You can all wait there in safety," she heard
herself say. "I shall return with others."

Her passengers, dumb with horror, obeyed. As
the beggar poled the boat away Zaryas looked
back, and saw them huddled in the rain.

Gradually a makeshift rescue was organized.
Small boats threaded the streets of drowned
Mishbil to ferry the living away. The patient
dead had to wait. The granaries stood deep in
water, but foods that could take wetting were
salvaged—sealed jars of pickled fruit, stoppered
bottles of oil.

Darkness came quickly, limiting the world to
the merciful circle that torchlight cast on the
restless water. "Further search must wait for
morning ," Zaryas acknowledged unwillingly. No
one dared relax in such buildings that still stood,
for they might fall in the night. So everyone
slept where they could outdoors in the rain—in
the boats, or on the little mud islands that once
had been a house. Zaryas found her slice of boat-
deck an entirely satisfactory couch.

Chapter 12: 21 Ynnem

The dawn was dreadful. Sullen clouds still wept over the city. As when the sword severs the hand the shock of loss had numbed all pain at first. Only with the light did the bereaved begin to mourn. The sobs and cries wound themselves horribly through Zaryas' dreams. She had been too tired to notice her bodily discomforts; being soaked through had become second nature. So she woke gradually. For a moment, half-awake, she was able to tell herself that it had all been a dreadful nightmare. She could leap out of bed and escape into the pleasant daytime world. Then she opened her eyes, and knew the dream terrors had conquered day. The water that is life had transmogrified into death.

Morning brought messengers from the outlying villages. The torrential rains had carved gullies in the dry soil and eroded hills into nothing. The very face of the land had altered. The canals were in ruins, their sides fallen in and their courses choked with silt. The new-sprouted barley had not rooted itself deeply enough to withstand the flood. The crops had washed away.

Now that starvation was truly imminent, no one seemed to care. The haggard faces of the living were more ghastly than those of the peaceful dead. Without surprise Zaryas recognized the wan hope in the eyes of those around her—the realization that death is kinder than life. A sweet lassitude, an urge to simply lie down in the turbid waters and quench life's flame, lay like a pall over the makeshift encampment.

In vain Zaryas tried to recapture yesterday's defiance. Mere instinct had fueled her then. "The cornered cat fights for life," she quoted to herself. Now like an over-burdened donkey in a sulk her weary mind refused to haul the load. Every hope she had nurtured had washed away yesterday; the new Shan King would very probably depose her from office for gross mismanagement. She wondered if the dam and its collapse had trebled the deluge's damage, or only doubled it.

The last of the salvaged provisons was cobbled together into a scanty meal. Zaryas warmed her hands round a mug of tea made from leaves used once already. Doggedly she tallied the survivors. There were about a hundred here. Surely there were others; searchers must be despatched to gather them together. Everyone must be moved to shelter on higher ground until the water went down. The dozens of pieces of the problems hung limp in her hands. Once they would have scurried to join each other in solutions. But the gray

sky and the gray dirty water besieged the little
encampment, smothering hope.

The plaiv tell that rulers ought to feel with
their folk. This is true, Zaryas knew, but like all
plaiv it is not completely true. Her duty was also
to breast the storm, to win through to calmer
waters and then guide her people there. Without
the force of her will to drive them out of despair
the people of Mishbil would perish. Yet even
responsibility's lash did not cast out her dispirit.
The effort of rebuilding seemed hardly worth-
while. Perhaps it would be fairer to resign immediately, and take her bad luck with her. She
had done little good for Mishbil so far.

Then the overcast was assaulted, not in a sor-
tie from the desperate defenders, but from without. The drizzle faltered. A patch of angry cloud
low in the east faded to lilac, then white, as it
thinned. Golden spears of sunlight pierced and
dissolved the weakened spot. The cheerful, ordinary light poured down so that Mishbil looked
homelike once more, though a little worse for
wear.

The very ground seemed to firm up under
Zaryas' bare feet. Of course she could not resign.
That would surrender Mishbil to its besiegers.
Farmers and fishermen believe always in the
next crop, the next cast of the net. The crazy
resilience of the gambler, who knows the bad
luck must someday turn, rose in her. Though the
shining-new discovery would soon be overlaid by
living Zaryas sensed she had stumbled on a fun-
damental truth. She, and all the Shan, gambled

or played Thumbprint for the same reasons kittens chase string—the amusement schools mind and will. How else could one practice risk and loss and endurance of spirit?

Her tea had grown cold. Defiantly Zaryas drained the mug anyway, and rose from her seat. The survivors were gathered round salvaged braziers, not trying to dry their clothes but simply warming themselves. Zaryas climbed up onto the prow of a dinghy, so that she could be seen. "The storm is over!" she announced. "All our gods be thanked!" The power of the new-lit torch—to pass fire on to others—was hers. With a sense of picking up an old, well-loved tool she continued, "The first thing to do is move, out of this wet. We shall set up a temporary camp—"

The renascence of her own spirit absorbed her so that she did not notice the silence. Then someone interrupted her. "No." She turned. A ragged, muscular man had risen from his seat—Torver-lis Melekirtsan. "We have followed you, Princess," he said quietly. "And where has it gotten us? Xerlanthor no doubt is gone where he cannot see what he has wrought. But is this devastation not partially your work too?"

"That's right," someone else chimed in. "All this comes of meddling with magi. The gods didn't approve of that, and cursed us."

"No, it was the Dragon, everyone knows you can't tame one—"

A babble of argument rose up on all sides. Zaryas clenched her hands and breathed deep. If the hurt made her lose control all would be lost.

"Quiet!" She made her voice harsh and loud. "The Shan King made me his viceroy. Only his successor may remove me. Dare you usurp his office?" She paused—it was a rhetorical question, but she wanted the sense of sacrilege to sink in. "On Mid Summer Day the new King shall be crowned. No doubt he will read your hearts and heed your pleas. The blame for these disasters shall be fixed. But until then, I rule. There is too much to be done; Mishbil cannot be pilotless."

The people were silent, but Zaryas sensed they would obey. She wondered if the captain of the lost *Silver Gull* had felt like this—so bruised and rejected. But the Shan adore quarrels and petty conflict. However painful the confrontation had been to her, it had certainly burned off some of the despair that hung over the camp. "If they want me out, they'll have to survive to do it," she told herself grimly.

Here and there across ravaged Mishbil that day islands of refugees signaled with smoke or flags. Like harvesters gathering in the shocks of grain, rescue boats slowly ferried groups to dry land. Zaryas made the Five Larches tavern a temporary headquarters, since it had not fallen and was close by on solid ground. The complex of stone-lined canals was gone, swept away or buried in silt. The farmers were dead or fled and the tavern's cellars and kitchens spoiled by water. But the sandy soil had drained quickly, and at least there was no longer a crop to be trampled. Soon a newcomer would have thought the temporary city quite sizeable. But Zaryas reckoned one in five in Mishbil had died.

There was no longer scope for nicety in food-supplies. Every living beast of burden had work before it. But Zaryas ordered the drowned donkeys and dogs cut up and salted at once before the meat should spoil. What was left of the Butchers' Guild protested, "Donkeys are notoriously tough eating! And dogs are undignified, not a traditional viand!"

Zaryas retorted, "If Viris isn't merciful we may yet be reduced to poaching rats!" This prospect so crushed the butchers they hastened to devise a brine for donkey-haunches, by boiling down sea water.

Only the fishing industry had survived unhurt. With many prayers to Ennelith Sea-Queen the fleets were dispatched on the noon tide. Fearing profiteers Zaryas mandated a uniform price for all fish caught until other foodsources were recovered. To placate the fishermen she left actual distribution in their Guild's hands still, reserving only the right to inspect their accounts.

But the chief task that day was the rescue of the living and the disposal of the dead. The grimmer labor was hindered by Viridese traditions: the honorable dead are properly sent off to the Deadlands in light wooden boats, laden with tinder and gifts, then towed out to sea and set afire. From the twin doors of fire and water no ghost returns to the land of the living.

Now the custom was unfeasible. Every seaworthy vessel was gone afishing. Nor was there dry wood to spare. And there was not time to allow the scattered survivors to find and gift their dead. The waters receded but Mishbil lay in the gravest danger now of plague. At last Zaryas ordered the corpses to be loaded onto river barges unsuited for seafaring.

"They shall be towed out to sea and scuttled," she promised the bereaved kin. "Ennelith will welcome them with song, and the White Queen shall not begrudge their informal arrival."

But as the corpses were stacked higher and higher, the barges took on an eerie resemblance to the firewood cargoes that used to come downriver. Mourners at the barges had to bid farewell to their dead quickly, before they were overlaid by yet more corpses.

Most pitiful of all were the many who still searched, father for children, brother for brother, wife for husband, not knowing where their loved ones waited—in some outpost of survivors, or on the barges. It was hopeless to ask the exhausted body crews, almost as hopeless to wait by the makeshift river-pier and scan each corpse as it was carted aboard.

But all that day Zaryas heard the murmur of fearful, muted queries from the muddy gravel-spit beside the pier. "A lad of eight years, in a purple weskit?" "My cousin was a very plump man, quite notably plump, with a bald spot, surely you must remember if you saw him? Well, would a little present stimulate memory? No?" "You haven't come across an elderly lady ... silver locket around her neck?"

There was probably no place where she would be more unwelcome. Zaryas was tempted to go down anyway. If she could communicate her sorrow and sympathy it might well smooth her future in Mishbil, when she was no longer princess-viceroy. And while she was there she might watch for a solid red-clad corpse, a drowned magus. But there were too many other things she had to do. Duty must prevail over both her political future and personal quests. Still, she knew the people would never understand, and probably never forgive her.

The Sun set that evening into a great bank of rosy cloud. The leveling scarlet light tinted the unruly Bilcad and washed cheerful color over the odorific mud-flats that had once been the streets. The waters ebbed swiftly out of the sandy soil. But the destruction they had wrought would take a generation to set right.

Zaryas worked far into the night, determined to go as far as possible toward recovery. With a ruthless efficiency she saw to it that everyone in her care got a hot meal and a dry place to sleep. But it hurt when her efforts were accepted coldly, in an attitude that said they were no longer services exchanged but payments due. She had known she would be liable for all the last year's wasted labor. But no one could have foreseen this dreadful debt as well. "It's mine, so I'll have to carry it," she told herself. She had never known how important her people's love had been.

Only one of the funeral-barge workers had a kind word. "You are our own tempest," he offered shyly. "Our own answer to the Dragon's wrath."

Zaryas was touched. Gruffly she replied, "Be sure to wash well before you start in on this," and handed him a bowl of stew.

"It's rancid," he objected.

Zaryas leaned over the kettle and tasted a spoonful. Though the chunks of meat had stewed all day they were still stringy. No spices had been available to mask the unusual flavor of donkey. "That's just the way donkey tastes," she said.

"How do you know?"

"I'm certain of it," she said firmly. To the east new-lit torches reflected in the flooded lowlands to double the flickering points of light. "Those must be a new lot of survivors—don't eat up all that stew."

"No fear," the worker grumbled.

The new arrivals stumbled in the darkness as they climbed uphill. They were greeted with cries of welcome by friends and relatives. Under cover of the noise the leader of the rescue team drew Zaryas aside. "My lady," he said, "we rescued a magus also."

Very timidly Zanyas asked, "Is it Xerlanthor?"

The leader—a thickset man old enough to be her father—scowled at her. "Of course not, my lady." Then, more kindly, he added, "If he's drowned, my lady, it's his good fortune and ours too. You're well shut of him."

Of course people blamed Xerlanthor most of all. With the best of intentions his work had magnified the impact of the natural disaster. Now

Zaryas realized how easy it would be to load all
the blame for the catastrophe onto him. He would
never have abandoned his dam, and so was surely
dead. Would he have wished her to fall with
him?

With an effort she wrenched her turbulent
thoughts back to the present. "Who is this magus
then?" she demanded. "Where is he?"

He puffed out his chest with pride. "I don't
know which he is, but here he comes."

Zaryas watched in stunned silence as Xantallon
trudged up into view. His red lappeted cap was
gone and soggy red remnants of his robe cloaked
his tall frame. But most unexpectedly his hands
were bound behind his back. His magic mirror
and thick-glass staff were carried by a woman
warrior, who eyed the unfortunate magus with a
cold, wary gaze.

"How dare you?" Zaryas gasped. "There isn't
a scrap of malice in any magus born!" How could
she not have seen that transferring blame to
Xerlanthor's dead shoulders might damn the magi
also? Hastily she continued, "Our only hope of
rebuilding Mishbil lies with the Order of Magi.
So let us not have any more of these unreasoning
grudges!" And taking refuge in action she borrowed a knife—she had lost her own yesterday—
and cut Xantallon's bonds.

"I'm not really hurt," the magus said kindly.
"It was a typical gesture, dramatic but painless."
He rubbed his chafed wrists and added, "Though
I'd appreciate my wand again, and the mirror

too. I was terrified every moment that she'd lose one or the other in the mud.''

At Zaryas' imperious gesture the magic tools were returned. "How can you bear this so calmly?" she asked. "They might have killed you."

"Oh, I doubt it," Xantallon said. "Anyway, magi espouse moderation. Is that stew? . . . if we bear our loss of credibility with patience it becomes less vexing."

"Is that all you can say?" With unsteady hands Zaryas ladled out a bowlful of stew. "Do you feel no pang then for the deaths, the destruction?"

Xantallon took a spoonful of stew, grimaced, and wiped his limp mustache. "Surely," he said. "But in moderation only. After all, what has happened can't be altered. Our duty will be not to weep, but work."

Without answering Zaryas got up and strode away. No wonder her people had been outraged by this infuriating calm. Events had been immoderate, her own warm heart cried. Surely they should be met with vehemence. She bit her lip as the bitter grief for Xerlanthor rose up in her. He would have felt as she did, though magi ought not. Even if she could it would be cruel to wish him back, to endure guilt and disdain and the inevitable formal inquiries. She would have to bear that for him, being the stronger. She hid her hands in her face to hide the tears. "They are right, my love," she muttered to herself. "You are happier dead. But never again will I find another like you."

Chapter 13: 24 Ynnem

In three days it was possible to descend into the city proper again. The Sun drew up wisps of vapor from the oozy dark mud that overlay everything. Uprooted trees and foundered buildings choked the slippery streets. Tangles of broken stalks and greenery here and there in the muck revealed themselves to be water lilies, torn out of their pools and pots by the rushing water. Zaryas directed these desolate remnants to be picked over—water-lily roots, dried and pounded, make a very fair flour.

Already the warm wet air was thick with the stench of death. There were too many drowned vermin and small beasts to dispose of in a day or even a week. Though personal cleanliness is a national pastime the Viridese are casual about streetcleaning. But everyone in the advance party was revolted at Mishbil's state now. "From city to flotsam heap in a day," Zaryas remarked.

The overflow sluice for the Eye Pool had been clogged by uprooted water lilies. Zaryas set a

few of her followers to clear them out. The viceroy's offices were still ankle-deep in water but
for a wonder had not fallen. Zaryas sent the
party on and waded in to fetch out a change of
clothing. The outer offices were desolate. All the
record-scrolls were soaked and illegible. The floor
sagged so that the shelves had fallen. Perhaps
the parchment could be whitened and reused.
The gray and greenish water stains on the crum-
bling plaster looked like sly, mocking faces. Zaryas
abandoned the chaos and went through into the
courtyard.

To her left the graceful colonnade had collapsed, the columns' foundations undermined by
water. She clambered over the heaps of broken
roof-tiles and rafters that had spoiled the oval
fountain pool. The second gate, to her surprise,
still stood proud in its wall. But the sudden
damp had warped its frame, and Zaryas wres-
tled with the latch for some minutes before giving up and climbing the wall beside the gate.

It was an easy climb—the planting-pockets gave
her toeholds—but she was uneasily aware that
the earth might not have finished settling. So
many things that had once been solid and safe
had fallen. This wall also might not bear her
weight. So she did not linger on the tiled wall-
top to survey her ruined domain, but slid quickly
down with the help of a nearby tree.

The guest wing had partially fallen but her
own chambers were intact. She opened the door
and gasped as an enormous brown rat leaped out
over her foot to skitter away. The cellars must

still be flooded. Nervously she listened for more
rats before tiptoeing inside. Puddles still lay here
and there on the mosaic floor, but otherwise her
home looked quite as usual. With renewed confidence she banged the door to and skipped down
the hall.

To her annoyance the bedchamber level was
still awash. Clothes in the lower cupboards were
ruined, but from an upper shelf she pulled a
warm quilted-linen jacket that did not yet reek
of mildew, and a hat made of blue-lacquered
straw. Zaryas set the hat on her head and was
rummaging for some leggings when a splash reso-
nated from the hall. "Viris curse these rats," she
muttered, and fumbled in the back of the cup-
board for her sword. She drew the blade from its
sheath, turned, and froze.

At the bottom of the five steps stood a man in
a dark tattered cloak. She could neither move
nor speak until he croaked, "Zaryas?"

"Xerlanthor!" Jacket and weapon fell splashing to the floor as she ran. The blue hat tumbled
off to float away upside-down as she threw herself into his arms. "Oh, you're real, you're alive!"

She felt a tear run down her neck as he mum-
bled into her hair, "I thought you hated me too,
for a moment."

"Never!" She hugged him tight to feel the
warmth and solidity she had thought lost against
herself. But his hands and face were cold as a
corpse, and his damp garments seemed to hold
no heat at all. She doubted he had slept or eaten
since the flood. She kissed the cheek against hers

and tasted salt. He wept almost soundlessly, from some source deep within. The painful sobs rose faster and faster, so that his solid frame shook in her arms. She heard the advance party halloing for her outside, but could not leave Xerlanthor in such a pass. Suddenly a head popped into view at the top of the stair.

"Is that a refugee?" Torver called down.

"Yes," Zaryas called back. "I mean, no. I don't need help, go on ahead."

Torver stared doubtfully down at them before going away. Zaryas feared he recognized Xerlanthor. She could not bear to expose him just yet to the unjust, inevitable calumny that awaited him. Everything had altered so terribly she hungered for some inviolate spot to rest in. Then she knew what to do. "Come, my dearest," she whispered. "Let's go up and see if the little balcony is dry."

By the time they emerged from the narrow dark stairway into the day Xerlanthor was calm. But in the mild sunshine his face wore such a ravaged, exhausted look that Zaryas was frightened. She lowered the trap-door so there would be room to sit, and asked, "However were you spared? Rumor had it you were drowned, for certain."

"I should have." He stared unseeing up at the hazy sky. "The overflow spillways were inadequate, I knew it as soon as I arrived at the Neck."

"Not your fault," Zaryas said stoutly. "You couldn't have known." But he did not seem to hear her.

"There was not time," he said. "With herognomers to turn the weather, hydromants to delay the torrents, geomancers to reinforce the work, I could have saved it. But there was not time. The water was already so high, thundering down into the sluice until it overwhelmed the channel."

He spoke as if he were frozen in the fearful recollection. Zaryas said, "We knew, here, when the dam broke. There was a wave. . . ."

He looked at her with a wide, fixed stare. "Do you remember those big facing stones? Those were the first to go. The lip of the dam was never designed to withstand such a current. You could hardly see the first block fall from the top, because of the rain. But you could hear it—the change in the current, because under the granite is earth mixed with rock . . . After that the end was quick."

She waited. When he did not continue she asked, "Is nothing left then?"

"The stones and gravel choke the Bilcad channel," he said, "but nothing impedes the Dragon anymore." He covered his face with his hands. The nails were dirty and broken, as if he had in the final extremity tried to hold the dam up with his own strength alone. "You can say it is not my fault. That is only partly true. When the dam broke and released the backed-up water the torrent rose higher than nature would ever have brought it."

Zaryas could not deny it. She had no word of comfort to offer. In a whisper he added, "I meant to be a savior. How did I destroy so much?"

His pain brought a lump to Zaryas' throat, but

she swallowed it down. "You mustn't despair," she said. "Let's look forward, not back. We still need your help."

He stared. "Your people would still trust me?"

"I don't know," Zaryas hedged. There was no point in telling him they no longer trusted her either. "But *I* still trust you. You are still the best geomancer in Mishbil. We shall need another water system, in time perhaps even another dam—"

"No," he interrupted. "The first cost me too dear."

"Then canals," she insisted. "Since we must redig them we can do it right this time, the way Xantallon wanted." Too late she realized mention of that name was perhaps imprudent. She hurried on, tripping in her eagerness over the words to relight the spirit that matched her own. "We mustn't despair, I discovered we mustn't despair. It's a matter of practice, you can learn how not to give in. You can drop out of Thumbprint games if you lose too much, but not out of living. You don't have a choice, you have to put down another stake. What else is there? There's nothing out there."

He stared at her. "That has nothing to do with me. I don't gamble."

Swiftly she changed her argument. "Nature herself endures disaster and recovers from it," she said. "Don't the magi coax the natural order to obey? Well, this will be simpler. Mishbil will recover from this, I know it will. All we need to do is help."

He rose but the tiny balcony allowed only three paces back and forth. "The Master Magus told you that," he said. "It sounds just like him. But he was wrong. The magi, the priestesses, the King, we're all wrong. The gods are not kind, as we were told, but malevolent. Nature is their weapon against us. Your endurance and gallantry are wasted."

His bitter words seemed almost to twist and crumble the kindly sunlit world around her. Through the livid cracks thus formed grinned another, demonic face. "Everything has two sides, you know," Xerlanthor continued cruelly. "We delude ourselves, averring that things are not necessarily good as opposed to bad. Then we further blind ourselves by regarding only the most pleasant aspect of everything. They are wrong when they advise a single eye and a single heart at a time. One has to contemplate both sides, and so grasp the unified whole."

For a moment the words weighted her down. Dark cold water forced itself into her, evil twiggy branches held her down. But she had won that fight once, and doubt no longer had real power over her. Old habits of common sense and plain thought reasserted themselves and heated her blood. She answered with vehemence. "If the gods are so vile, which I don't concede for a moment, then I wouldn't give them the satisfaction. I'd fight to the last breath. Wherever did you get this odd fancy? One can't see both aspects of anything at once, any more than both faces of a coin show at the same time."

Xerlanthor's face was red but his voice was even. "I've discovered a different truth from you, then. I find that working for others is sterile. When you succeed the crowd's applause is cheap, and when you fail they tear you apart. You say one mustn't give up. Well, I shan't. There are hundreds of fields of inquiry that the Order never takes up. It's too busy servicing canals and aligning houses for luck. So I will explore them, and no longer pour my heart out on water systems— seek my own approval and applause."

One part of her knew then with terrible certainty that he was lost forever. Like so many of Mishbil's houses Xerlanthor had not been founded solidly enough. But her other side refused to admit its loss, and dashed about hunting for the key—the key to open the dark door and let Xerlanthor back out into the sunlight. "Those of ability have to serve the common good," she argued. "Where else should they find scope for their talents?" Someday, she told herself, those words will return to damn me. But ignoring that possibility she continued, "I know my energies should be wasted, in any office but this. So too would you be, severed from your work in the Order."

Opposition, she ought to have remembered, merely hardened him. "I've shown I don't need magian help," he said. "Outside the Order I'd be free."

"You'd be lost—" A flanking movement, she thought. There must be a more vulnerable side, a chink to let me through—"At least, to me."

"So now we come to it," Xerlanthor said coldly. "If I don't stay obediently in my useful and customary slot you too will cast me out. Who then was using whom?"

He said it with hurtful intent, and that, more than the words themselves, brought tears to her eyes. But suddenly she knew what to say. "I would never cast you out. For I am with child—by you."

The watery sunlight showed his haggard face blank with astonishment. She paused but when he did not speak continued, "When the Mistress confirmed it I was delighted." Gently, casually, as one might steal up on a bird, she approached him. His arm was heavy for lack of a supporting will as she tucked it into her own. The skin was tight and clammy over his knuckles. "It seems there's an explanation for—"

With a sudden wrench that made her stagger Xerlanthor twisted out of her grasp. "Explanation!" he almost hissed. "What explanation could there be, but that you decided to be rid of me months ago!"

His rage took her by surprise. She smiled, hoping to laugh it off. Not until he raised a strong fist did she remember to be afraid.

The blow split the skin over her cheekbone and made red and yellow stars explode in her left eye. "Xerlanthor!" she cried. "Are you insane?" His fingers, so strong and clever, bored into her shoulder and neck. With an effort she relaxed in his grip, forcing her voice to be sensible and soothing. "You know that's nonsense, when have I had time for dalliance?"

Bronzen hands dug into her throat, choking off breath. Their strength was more terrifying than that of the tempest, for they were guided by a deliberate malice. The roar of blood in her ears drowned out Xerlanthor's words, but through dimming sight she saw his contorted face mouthing above her own. Years later she would wake from sleep and hear their message echo through her brain. The mocking fate that had undone him, the wasted love and labor and hope: he communicated all the fury and pain in words she could not hear, and more explicit language.

When Zaryas realized submission struck no chord in him she fought back, writhing to kick with booted feet. With a shout of justified anger he released her and struck out. She had lost her knife and now could not match his longer reach. She felt her face swell and her ribs crack. The friendly supporting wall at her back turned traitor, tilting to let her slide to the trap-door floor. From a great distance she sensed his knees on her chest and body, his sobbing breath in her ear.

Long after, Zaryas knew she lived because she hurt. It seemed too much trouble to live. If she lay here and died, likely no one would find her body for days. Vultures in plenty already haunted the sky; her clean-picked bones would cause no unseemly odor or disturbance.

But death does not come at a wish, and her body clung stubbornly to its life. Presently Zaryas became aware that the eye she could open saw brown spots on the whitewashed plaster parapet. Blood, of course—her own, dried in the Sun. It would have to be tidied up before the stain set. With a groan she hauled herself to a sitting position and took stock of the damage.

Her wrist and right hand would not work properly, and from their ache she thought a bone or two had gone. It hurt to breathe but her limbs seemed relatively sound. Without surprise she looked down to see pale bare skin, mottled with swelling bruises. Dully she wondered if he had raped her at the last, an ultimate perversion of all that had been before. But her body hurt too fiercely to testify on this point, and it made no difference anyway. Of course he was gone—over the parapet, or across the roofs, a wind-walker even now.

Shivering, she pried up the trap-door and tottered down the stair. Waves of sparkly black lapped round her feet, urging her to fall. When she reached the main floor she sat down to rest. A new and relentless pain was beginning to grind in her back and belly, and she feared she had taken some internal injury. Then it came to her. Whether because of the battering, the stresses of the last few days, or simply because her body now refused to have anything further to do with Xerlanthor, she was losing their child.

It seemed natural and right to her now to weep, where before it would have been a surrender. She lifted her voice and wailed like a child, hiding her face in her hands. Very much later she reflected wryly that it was the wisest thing she did that day. Almost instantly her cries drew answering calls and hurrying footsteps. People clattered up, exclaiming and questioning. Warm coverings cloaked her nakedness, and warm arms—Torver's, she thought—bore her up. "How did this happen?" he demanded in a voice that hurt her ears.

"A tumble down the stair?"

"No, these are marks of violence."

"My lady, who did this?"

The sparkling dark tide had risen quite high. Zaryas could no longer remember why she had feared it. "Xerlanthor," she whispered, and let herself go.

Chapter 14: Mid Summer Day

The survivors in Mishbil agreed that it was by Viris' mercy Norveth-ven had been spared to them. Most of the work to be done—cleaning the streets, disposing of the dead, rebuilding houses, replanting crops—could be done by anyone. But only the viceroy—and perhaps now her second also—could allocate supplies, set priorities, negotiate for aid. The remainder of the city's bonesetters and herbals had many casualties in their care. So Norveth used the miscarriage as an excuse to entrust Zaryas to the Sodality. "Since Ennelith struck the Princess down, let Ennelith heal her," he announced. This drastic eclipse of Zaryas' sun was melancholy, but it did supply opportunity for lesser lights to shine.

For some days Zaryas lay insensible as a slow fever scorched her. The world shrank to a narrow bed, and the sky to a warm quilt. The slow, twisting pain in her belly made her writhe and toss. Yet the throb of her ribs, and the splints on her arm, demanded stillness. "I can't please any

179

member of my body," she complained in a lucid moment.

"This will help." Gentle hands sponged her hot forehead with a cooling herbal infusion. Through blurry eyes Zaryas saw a familiar face, moon-colored in the light of a blue-shaded night lamp. There is no tradition of malevolent ghosts in Averidan, but in a guilty croak Zaryas asked, "Are you back from the Deadlands because I scamped your funeral?"

"Don't be silly," the Mistress said. "Bring some of that broth, Moryil. While she's awake the Princess should take some nourishment."

She's dead, Zaryas reflected sleepily. I must be dreaming. One never eats in dreams or marks time either, so she asked, "What day is it?"

"Mid Summer Day evening," the Mistress replied. "The first of Arbas. Today they crowned the new Shan King."

"Did they?" That was so undreamlike a statement Zaryas was startled. "Who was chosen?"

The Mistress took the bowl of barley broth and held out a spoonful. "You must eat," she commanded. "Your only care now is to get well."

The words were kindly meant, but Zaryas could not swallow a bite. When the new King deposed her, she would indeed be carefree.

The next day she recognized the room the moment she woke. Carven shutters were folded back from low, wide windows. Outside sapphire waves flung themselves tirelessly up a shining gravelly gold beach. The tide was all the way out, turning even as she watched, and its distant rhythm filled

the air. Her covers and pillows were linen of the
palest, most delicate blue. Her hurts no longer
pained her. It was easy to believe she had merely
dreamed the past week or so, until she sat up.
Then her tight-bound ribs throbbed in protest.
Carefully she lay back again. Memory returned
in so vivid a flood that she unwisely bit her lip,
and then winced at the pain.

Somehow she had lost everything. She remembered—if last night had not been a dream—that
yesterday had been Mid Summer Day. "A year,"
she said aloud. "That's all. I'm young, I can spare
a year." But as from some plaiv the words returned to her mind, "It cost me too dear." There
was an end to the contents of the largest purse.

With a sidewise sort of skip her mind rebounded
to Xerlanthor. Where was he now? Was he sorry?
Defiantly she sat up again, letting her pains re-
mind her and drive those thoughts away.

The carved cypresswood door opened. "Zaryas!"
the Mistress exclaimed. "You ought not rise
yet!"

Obediently she leaned back onto the pillows.
"I thought you were drowned," Zaryas said. The
tears she had not then dared to shed welled up
now. When the breakfast tray was set on her
knees she sobbed into her porridge.

The Mistress drew up a chair at the bedside,
but politely did not sit down until Zaryas was a
little calmer. Then she seated herself and said,
"The wave swept me down between the boats,
but by the Goddess' mercy it whirled me out
again into open water before I was crushed. I

clung to a raft of flotsam all night, and called myself fortunate."

Zaryas blew her nose, exhausted by her tears. The barley porridge was congealing in its bowl, but she took a spoonful anyway, knowing how hard it must have been to come by. The tough shreds of dark meat mixed in revealed themselves to be donkey rather than the usual fish. She choked down a mouthful and asked, "What has become of Mishbil?"

"I will only discuss affairs with you very briefly, Zaryas," the Mistress remarked, "because you must rest today. Your second, Norveth-ven, has taken over management."

She spoke in the sympathetic tone of one breaking unhappy news. But very calmly Zaryas replied, "I'm glad of it. Someone must care for my people if I cannot."

"He intends to replace you as viceroy," the Mistress said.

"Only the Shan King can do that," Zaryas said. "But I expect he will. His Shan Majesty wouldn't want a failure to represent him."

"This wasn't your fault!" the Mistress burst out. Then with some calmness she continued, "But if you have accepted your lot I ought not excite you."

"My heart feels battered numb," Zaryas confessed. "I hardly care at all.

"That's because you're still ill." She smoothed and plumped the pillows for Zaryas with an expert hand, and lifted the tray away. "Should you like to sleep some more?"

Zaryas nodded, and drew the quilts up. Her problems clamored for attention. Never before had she been slow to attack them. But she could not begin until her body obeyed her. She must sleep, and regain health. All that day she slipped in and out of slumber, rocked on the sound of the waves. That night she slept deep, freed from the hot weight of fever.

The next morning she felt almost herself again. She threw back the covers. Her legs were shaky with disuse, but as she leaned on the windowsill she felt the blood course through her veins with new vigor.

She could not live with the Sodality forever. For the first time she considered her future, and found it a gloomy prospect. The Shan King's bureaucratic appointments are nearly always made for life. The family dye business had been made over to her cousins more than five years ago. Would they welcome her return? They were able managers and needed no help. There is no denying ties of blood, Zaryas consoled her sore, proud heart. They would have to make the best of her.

The door burst open and a young novice hurried in. "Thank Viris you're awake, my lady," the lass said, panting. "Here are clothes. You have callers."

"Who could they be?" Zaryas wondered.

But the novice shook her head. "The Mistress greeted them, and sent me to tell you." She had brought an armload of miscellaneous clothing snatched at random from some store-cupboard.

Zaryas chose an amber-colored linen robe and an ebony silk under blouse. There were no shoes—leather would be a rarity in Mishbil for the next few months—but the robe's embroidered hems came down far enough to hide the lack. When Zaryas was dressed, the novice scurried away to inform her Mistress.

Then Zaryas remembered her hair. So far as she could tell it had not been combed through since the deluge. Quickly she unbraided it and began dragging a comb through the snarls. The door opened before she was ready. The shock, when she looked up to see the solid red-clad figure across the room, was so great the wooden comb slipped from her hand and clattered across the tile floor.

"My dear princess, I'm so sorry." The Master Magus moved quickly to support her. "You must lie down—no? At least sit, here." He hooked a chair forward with one foot.

Zaryas caught her breath. "Xarlim, I'm so glad to see you," she said. "Whenever did you arrive?" His companion stepped forward to pick up the comb. Zaryas did not recognize him—a thin young man, barely out of boyhood, with a pale unhappy face, slouching in preposterous amethyst silks.

"This morning," the Magus said. "His Majesty and I sailed directly after the coronation. Shan Eisen, let me present to you the viceroy of Mishbil, Zaryas-yu Borletsikan."

Zaryas was too surprised to be tactful. "They chose you?" Then she blushed with embarrassment. The Collegium of Counsellors invariably chose a wise, just monarch. As she had told Xerlanthor once, such mysteries must be arcane, hidden.

The Shan King did not seem offended. "I am not yet inured to kingship," he said in a kind tone, "so of course I don't look a king. Fortunately, I have credentials." With a long pale hand he gestured a servant forward. From a gold-bound casket he lifted the Crystal Crown, emblem and talisman of the Shan King, and set it on his head. For a moment its white glow lent Eisen an unearthly glory. Before Zaryas had time for surprise it was gone. Only the smudges of weariness were a little more noticeable under the Shan King's eyes.

"We hurried because tidings of Mishbil were so dreadful," the Magus said. "I've been in touch with magi here by mirror."

"Then you know all," Zaryas said. Too late now she realized how lucky the captain of the *Silver Gull* had been. He had not had to formally resign his office. She swallowed, and steadied her voice. "I know the Shan do not favor rulers tainted with failure. Do you come to depose me?"

"If Mishbil's welfare demands it I will not hesitate," the Shan King said. His voice rang with a new confidence. "But I am not yet satisfied that is wise. This is an unofficial visit so far, you understand me. Tell her, magister."

The Magus took off his peaked red cap and scratched the round bald spot underneath. "Of course the flood was devastating, terrible. One

expects chaos, especially when records are ruined. But when buildings are looted something is
deeply wrong."

"Looted?" Zaryas asked sharply.

"A little too energetically salvaged, perhaps,"
the Shan King suggested.

"The fact of the matter is, my dear Zaryas,"
the Magus said, "things are not proceeding well
in Mishbil. Even after allowing for the flood's
aftermath. The city is drifting. The truth is,
managers of drive and vision are perennially in
short supply."

Zaryas stared attentively at the Magus. But
she was acutely aware the Shan King's scrutiny
was focused on her. Was he hearing testimony
she had no tongue for? Judging her by criteria
she did not know she supplied? She felt an impulse to cover herself, to hide from him, but
stifled it. The lord of the Shan is always just and
wise. Though she did not know how that was
managed, she trusted in it.

"These incidents are only one example," the
Magus was saying. "Take the Fishers' Guild, for
instance. Can you believe, with such shortages,
that they've dared to quintuple their prices?"

"What? Norveth should have kept an eye on
them," Zaryas snapped. "When things slide so
far only a lapidation or two will mend them.
There's no excuse for such laxness on Norveth's
part." Zaryas quite forgot the Shan King's piercing gaze as she tapped her bare feet on the floor.
What on earth could Norveth have been thinking
of? Why the populace must be starving, living on

mud and grilled vermin. Now she thought of it the Sodality had not yet served her seafood, their favorite. "Norveth's sister-in-law's family owns a fishing fleet," she said frowning. "Now, I wonder—"

She paused, pricked with guilt. The slight smile on the Shan King's face was unreadable; its appraising judicial air seemed odd on such a young, unformed countenance. His dark eyes glinted at her from beneath lowered lids as he murmured, "Indeed. How diligent of Varim. . . ." In a clearer tone he added, "I think, Zaryas, that if we can persuade the people to accept you again, no change in administration will be necessary. As the Magus says, good viceroys are rare."

For a moment Zaryas was at a loss, from surprise and delight. Then she got up and bowed before the King, her unbound hair brushing the floor. "My gifts in your service, Your Majesty," she said—the ritual thank-words. "But—my people cast me off."

"They have missed you as much as you missed them," the King declared. "And the cause of your present illness must be made more widely known."

"Is it not?" Zaryas could have sworn she had mentioned Xerlanthor to her rescuers.

"I should say, properly known," said the King. "Your sufferings and losses cannot fail to rouse sympathy." Zaryas' hand crept up to feel her face. She had forgotten she was so battered. She wondered how the Shan King had learned so quickly to manage Viridese rumor.

"You intend then to transfer all blame to Xerlanthor," the Magus said.

The Shan King nodded. "I'm afraid it must be either him or yourself," he said to Zaryas.

She said nothing. The Shan King was wrong, she realized. For her the choice was between her love and her work. Perhaps it had always been so, and she had never noticed. Now the moment had come to say the final word that would dissever Xerlanthor from her eternally. And she could not do it. The love she had borne for him suddenly shook her violently. "What will become of him then?" she cried. "Magister, shall the Order cast him off utterly?"

"He has cast himself out," the Magus said sadly. "Neither word nor sign of him has been found in Averidan this past week. And magi, as you know, can see far. He is no longer one of us, no longer, perhaps, even one of the Shan. He's gone."

"You've scried? Consulted his family?" But she could read on the Magus' face that inquiry had been fruitless. She demanded of the King, "How can it be just, to fasten the work of nature onto one guiltless?"

"The magus Xerlanthor was not irreproachable," the Shan King pointed out. "I understand your feelings, princess, but you must also allow me to salvage what I can from the wreck."

As it had once before, the honorific steadied her. The other side of her had a chance to speak. Xerlanthor was lost not because he failed but because he despaired. Could such a one have any part of her? All of a sudden she could not believe it. "It must be as you say, then," she slowly assented. The last barrier hurdled, with more energy she said, "Perhaps the best move would be to make Your Majesty's visit an official one. Would you wish to stay at the viceroy's house?"

"I would be pleased to," the Shan King said.

"Let's go over, then," Zaryas said. "I'll wager Norveth has had the house tidied up very well. After all, he wants to live there."

The Magus frowned as Zaryas rummaged through the pile of clothing for a cloak. "Ought you to leave the Sodality's care?" he asked.

"I have work to do," she replied absently. With regret she rubbed one bare foot on the instep of the other. "I wonder if the Mistress will mind lending me one more pair of shoes."

Appendix

The Viridese year begins on Mid Summer Day—the most fortunate day of the most fortunate season. A few days preceding both it and Mid Winter Day are counted separately from the twelve months, which are 30 days each. These are named with four seasonal syllables—'spring,' 'summer,' and so on—plus three ordinal suffixes, 'early,' 'middle,' and 'late.' Though days are also named and numbered their nomenclature is falling into disuse. So a year of the Shan would look like this:

Month
Arbas   1 Arbas being Mid Summer Day
Arhem
Arnep
Ekbas   Autumn equinox
Ekhem
Eknep
   2 days of Mid Year holiday: a time to think on the past, cast accounts, update genealogies, and pay taxes.
Olbas   1 Olbas being Mid Winter Day
Olhem
Olnep
Ynbas   Spring equinox
Ynhem
Ynnep
   3 or 4 days of holiday, devoted to parties, tidying house, and getting ready for the new year.

DAW

DAW BRINGS YOU THESE BESTSELLERS BY
MARION ZIMMER BRADLEY

☐ CITY OF SORCERY	UE1962—$3.50
☐ DARKOVER LANDFALL	UE1906—$2.50
☐ THE SPELL SWORD	UE2091—$2.50
☐ THE HERITAGE OF HASTUR	UE2079—$3.95
☐ THE SHATTERED CHAIN	UE1961—$3.50
☐ THE FORBIDDEN TOWER	UE2029—$3.95
☐ STORMQUEEN!	UE2092—$3.95
☐ TWO TO CONQUER	UE1876—$2.95
☐ SHARRA'S EXILE	UE1988—$3.95
☐ HAWKMISTRESS	UE2064—$3.95
☐ THENDARA HOUSE	UE1857—$3.50
☐ HUNTERS OF THE RED MOON	UE1968—$2.50
☐ THE SURVIVORS	UE1861—$2.95

Anthologies

☐ THE KEEPER'S PRICE	UE1931—$2.50
☐ SWORD OF CHAOS	UE1722—$2.95
☐ SWORD AND SORCERESS	UE1928—$2.95

NEW AMERICAN LIBRARY
P.O. Box 999, Bergenfield, New Jersey 07621

Please send me the DAW Books I have checked above. I am enclosing
$_____ (check or money order—no currency or C.O.D.'s).
Please include the list price plus $1.00 per order to cover handling
costs.

Name _____

Address _____

City _____ State _____ Zip Code _____
Allow 4-6 weeks for delivery

DAW

The really great fantasy books are
published by DAW:

Andre Norton

LORE OF THE WITCH WORLD	UE2012—$3.50
HORN CROWN	UE2051—$3.50
PERILOUS DREAMS	UE1749—$2.50

C.J. Cherryh

THE DREAMSTONE	UE2013—$3.50
THE TREE OF SWORDS AND JEWELS	UE1850—$2.95

Lin Carter

DOWN TO A SUNLESS SEA	UE1937—$2.50
DRAGONROUGE	UE1982—$2.50

M.A.R. Barker

THE MAN OF GOLD	UE1940—$3.95

Michael Shea

NIFFT THE LEAN	UE1783—$2.95
THE COLOR OUT OF TIME	UE1954—$2.50

B.W. Clough

THE CRYSTAL CROWN	UE1922—$2.75